Sleigh Bells at Moonglow

Sleigh Bells at Moonglow

A Moonglow Christmas Novella

Deborah Garner

Cranberry Cove Press

Cranberry Cove Press, PO Box 1671, Jackson, WY 83001, United States

Cover design by Mariah Sinclair | www.mariahsinclair.com

Library of Congress Catalog-in-Publication Data Available

Garner, Deborah

Sleigh Bells at Moonglow / Deborah Garner—1st United States edition 1. Fiction 2. Woman Authors 3. Holidays

p. cm.

978-1-952140-34-1 (paperback)

978-1-952140-36-5 (hardback)

Printed in the United States of America 10 9 8 7 6 5 4 3 2

The Paige MacKenzie Mystery Series
Above the Bridge
The Moonglow Café
Three Silver Doves
Hutchins Creek Cache
Crazy Fox Ranch
Sweet Sierra Gulch

The Moonglow Christmas Series
Mistletoe at Moonglow
Silver Bells at Moonglow
Gingerbread at Moonglow
Nutcracker Sweets at Moonglow
Snowfall at Moonglow
Yuletide at Moonglow
Starlight at Moonglow
Joy at Moonglow
Evergreen Wishes at Moonglow
Angels at Moonglow
Sleigh Bells at Moonglow

The Sadie Kramer Flair Series
A Flair for Chardonnay
A Flair for Drama
A Flair for Beignets
A Flair for Truffles
A Flair for Flip-Flops
A Flair for Goblins

A Flair for Shamrocks
A Flair for Vegas

Other Titles
Cranberry Bluff
Sweet Treats
More Sweet Treats

For my mother,
who always made holidays special for us.

Chapter One

Mist slipped onto a stool at the kitchen counter, letting the flowing skirt of her embroidered dress fall softly to the side. Next to her, Rain sat in a high chair, dressed in a romper with identical embroidery. With brown hair of similar color and texture as Mist's, coupled with matching hazel eyes and a slender face, there was no doubt she was Mist's daughter.

Mist took a sip of peppermint tea and watched Rain take a sip of her pretend tea. It was hard to believe the sweet girl was almost eighteen months old already. Time was passing quickly, too quickly. She had heard mothers say this before, but now she understood.

Opening the hotel's registration book, she looked over the upcoming arrivals, feeling the exciting sensation that she did every Christmas. Having guests come to the Timberton Hotel for the holiday season was always a treat, and she looked forward to those both new and returning. She considered them all friends, all family, even those she had yet to meet.

Betty, the hotelkeeper and Mist's dear friend and mother figure, entered the kitchen, poured herself a cup of coffee that

Mist had already prepared for her, and took a seat across from her at the counter.

"Good morning, Rain," Betty said, smiling when she received a semi-clear response back from the young girl. "And good morning to you, of course, Mist. I see you have the reservation book open. It's going to be a busy few days, isn't it? Like always at this time of year, which is so delightful." Betty took a sip of coffee and waved at Rain, who giggled and waved back.

"Delightful indeed," Mist replied. "It might be our busiest and most exciting Christmas season so far." I'm looking forward to everything—guests, decorations, meals in the café, music... so many things."

"And the special event this year," Betty said. "I can barely wait!"

Mist smiled, proud that Michael had suggested a sleigh ride activity. And like many such ideas, it caught on as others in town added input. By the time the round of additional suggestions was complete, the result was a sensational endeavor that no one had seen before, certainly not in Timberton or other local areas: a sleigh ride through the forest that surrounded the town with "station" stops along the way. And with ticket sales—kept to a moderate price that people could afford—supporting a variety of local programs, including the library's literacy project, it had become a wonderful support of the town. The hotel had purchased tickets for all the incoming guests as well as quite a few for those who were likely to pass it up for monetary reasons.

"Clive and Duffy have worked so hard on those stations," Betty said. "Thank goodness Duffy has all those woodworking tools."

"I know." Mist's eyes sparkled. "It's amazing. And I love the way they figured out a basic, rustic design that can be taken apart and used again in the future. Like a portable pergola."

Betty took another sip of coffee and then nodded toward the reservation book. "So who do we have coming this year?"

Mist ran her finger down the page. "Naturally we have Clara and Andrew. They never miss a Christmas here."

"Oh, I can't wait to hear their stories about this year's trip," Betty exclaimed. "They met up with the professor in London and stayed with his sister, Chloe, and his niece, Poppy."

"Yes, outside of the city, I believe, so they would have seen some of the English countryside." Mist stopped to think about this. She hadn't traveled much, but she'd always loved the idea of the small hamlets and cottages she'd heard about. It would be wonderful to hear the firsthand experiences of Clara and Andrew's visit to that area.

"Who else, aside from the regulars," Betty asked. "Michael and the professor will be here, of course."

"Yes," Mist said. "They are certainly regulars. We do have first-time guests, as always. Ivy Porter is one of them, a single mother with two daughters. She's coming from Santa Cruz, coincidentally where I went to college, possibly around the time I was there. I'm eager to meet her."

"How great! I'm sure you two will have things to talk about." Betty got up, refilled her coffee cup, and sat back down. "And the horses arrive today?"

Mist laughed, picturing horses checking into the hotel. "Tomorrow, but they'll stay at a barn outside of town. We don't have room for them here."

"Very funny." Betty grinned. "But the driver is staying with us."

Mist nodded. "Yes, Christine Hubbard. She's from Montana, just farther north, around Fort Benton. She'll check in tomorrow once she gets the horses settled in the barn."

"And who else? You mentioned someone from back east?"

"Yes, the Hudsons, Diana and Graham," Mist said,

checking the registration notes. "They're coming from New York."

Betty nodded. "Well, that's good. They'll be used to the snow, and there's no shortage of that this year."

Mist glanced out the window, noting, and not for the first time, that Betty was right. It had been an especially snowy December, which was welcome. Guests loved a white Christmas.

"I glanced at the book the other day," Betty said. "Looks like arrivals are spread out this time."

"Yes." Mist checked the book. "Some tonight, some tomorrow."

"No one on the twenty-third?"

"No," Mist said, "and it's a good thing, since we have your cookie exchange in the early afternoon and the sleigh rides start later. Plus a casual dinner, which is usual for the night before the big Christmas Eve feast. But that will be spread out so people can take a sleigh ride at different times. I'll start setting up dinner after the cookie exchange. It'll be a busy day."

"Yes, indeed!" Betty clapped her hands, and Rain did the same. "And speaking of Christmas Eve dinner, what's on this year's menu?"

"Something for everyone, I think." Mist retrieved a paper from a side counter and set it in front of Betty, who looked it over and then smiled.

Boeuf bourguignon
Lentil roast with balsamic onion gravy
Pear pomegranate salad
Roasted garlic butter fingerling potatoes
Honey-glazed butternut squash
Lemon quinoa with currants and dill

Rosemary focaccia
Gingerbread bundt cake with fresh whipped cream

"It looks wonderful, as always, Mist. I might have to indulge in an extra serving of the gingerbread bundt cake!"

Mist smiled. "Thank you. It should make for an elegant evening. The other evenings will be basic."

"Your idea of basic can be a little different from others' ideas of basic."

"Maybe I'll surprise you this year." Mist lifted Rain out of the high chair and held her casually on her hip.

Betty also stood up, laughing. "You surprise us every year, in fact, every day."

"Just as it should be," Mist said. She turned to Rain. "Isn't that right?" To which Rain answered with something that sounded quite close to the word *right*. Mist turned back to Betty. "You see? There are always surprises."

"You have a point," Betty said. "Both of you."

"Life is a mystery filled with the unexpected, " Mist said. "And we wouldn't want it any other way."

Chapter Two

A cacophony of noise greeted Mist as she stepped through the front door of Duffy's. The usual chatter of locals conversing with each other mixed with the sound of the cash register—Duffy insisted on using a vintage register that sang its own praises whenever ringing up a sale—and a blender in the soda fountain area, the latter a telltale sign that someone had chosen a shake over an ice-cream soda. But the additional noise not heard every day in the popular market—known more accurately as "an everything store"—came from the rear of the building.

Mist passed through the creative aisles that Duffy had originally set up when he built the store. Wooden crates and old-fashioned barrels held root vegetables, candy, and smaller packaged dry goods. Rustic shelving held heavier items or those too large for the smaller displays. Metal bins with varieties grains and nuts waited, scoops ready, for customers in need of bulk supplies.

Making a note of pecan halves that could come in handy

for one of the holiday meals planned for the café, Mist stepped into the back room, where she found Duffy and Clive engrossed in a woodworking project.

"Making another display pergola?" Mist asked as she watched the activity.

"Yep," Clive said, hammer in hand. "We're short one. At least we think we are. Maybe. We might be."

"That's right," Duffy added as if Clive had said something definitive. "And if we aren't, it won't hurt to have an extra."

Mist agreed they had a point. What had started as a plan for simple umbrellas for the sleigh ride stops had morphed into sturdy wooden structures that could protect those at the stops from winter elements. And it had been decided after much deliberation by Clive and Duffy to make them portable, able to be taken apart, stored, and reassembled for future events. It was a clever albeit ambitious project. But it would serve the community in the future. And if it took a sleigh ride to instigate it, that was fine. Big ideas often sprang from smaller ones.

"So that will make..." Mist mentally counted up the sleigh stops she knew were planned. "Six altogether?" Marge would have a station, Millie would have another, Sally had a plan for one, Ernie from Pop's Parlor planned to man another, Glenda from the Curl 'n' Cue would cover one, and Addison from Clive's gallery would handle the sixth. Each would have a treat for visitors who passed by.

"That's right," Duffy said. Clive nodded as shook one leg of the structure they were building. "Sturdy enough," he said to himself.

Mist knew there were technically two other stops. The sleigh ride would begin in front of the hotel and end at Duffy's, though neither of those required a wooden stand. So it was considered eight stops, two in town and six outside of town in a forest area. Her heart warmed at the thought of it all.

Timberton had never held such a unique event, and it guaranteed to create sweet holiday memories for those who participated.

"More paintings? Clive asked hopefully, glancing at a canvas tote bag that Mist held by her side.

"As requested." Mist lifted the bag in response to his question. "I'll drop them at the gallery on my way to Maisie's." She had spent the past few evenings creating a new design for the miniature four-by-four paintings she'd made for years. This one featured a bright red sleigh beneath a canopy of pine trees, an appropriate image for the current town activity. The paintings were a popular item for visitors to buy, and Clive and Mist tried to keep the gallery well stocked with them.

Leaving the men to their construction project, Mist continued her walk along Timberton's Main Street. The short stretch, just over two blocks, always enchanted her with its quaint shops and Western storefronts. This year was even more magical with white, twinkling lights, festive pine garlands, and windows offering holiday displays. Across the street, the town park boasted a community Christmas tree that Clayton and his fire crew decorated with lights. On snowy nights, it was worth bundling up and heading out just to see the tree beneath the falling snow. It was not unheard of for townsfolk, gathered there by chance in the early evenings, to break out in song.

Mist nodded to Addison, Clive's assistant, who was busy with a customer. The young woman had become an essential part of running the gallery. Mist headed to Clive's desk in the back of the shop and set the tote bag down. The dozen new paintings would help cover some customer requests and also add to the display on the gallery wall. The paintings, being small and affordable, were a popular item, especially with the many customers who would not be able to afford larger pieces of art.

Waving to Addison, Mist left the gallery and continued on to Maisie's Daisies. Maisie had become a dear friend over the years, always providing perfect flowers and greenery when needed. Over the past two years, they'd become even closer as their daughters began to grow up together. Maisie's eighteen-month-old Cora and Mist's seventeen-month-old Rain were destined to become close friends just like their mothers.

"Oh, perfect timing! I have everything you ordered!" Maisie exclaimed as Mist entered the small floral boutique. Maisie's short, cropped hair with streaks of green in it always made Mist smile. It matched her spunky personality just as her overalls and tie-dyed shirt did.

Maisie hurried into the back room and returned with two overflowing bundles of flowers held together by butcher paper and twine. She held them up to her nose to breathe in the fragrance and then set them on the counter.

"These are gorgeous!" Mist exclaimed, admiring the assortment of petite red roses, ivory orchids, red berries, baby's breath, and mixed greenery. "I know exactly how I'll arrange these."

"Did you find the little sleighs you were searching for?"

"I did," Mist said. She'd been thrilled to find basic wooden sleighs online, which she'd painted with cheerful holiday colors. They were small enough to serve as centerpieces in the café but large enough to hold an assortment of flowers. To make them a tiny bit fancier, Mist planned to add the tiniest bit of gold glitter once the arrangements were done.

"That'll be perfect for this year," Maisie said. "And adorable for future years if you use them again. Though you always come up with something new."

Mist nodded. "I think guests enjoy seeing new arrangements each year. I might donate these to a senior center. They could use them next season for a luncheon or other program."

"Great idea," Maisie said, looking up as the chime on the front door signaled the arrival of another customer.

"I'll leave you to attend to business," Mist said. "Thanks so much for a beautiful assortment." She gathered the floral bouquets into her arms and headed back to the hotel.

Chapter Three

Mist found Betty in the hotel kitchen, a pot of sugary mixture cooking on the stove and two large baking sheets set out on the counter.

"Beautiful flowers!" Betty exclaimed as she saw the delivery Mist had in her arms. "Maisie brought in some gorgeous ones this year. Like every year, of course!"

"Exactly." Mist set the flowers down on a side counter, ready to be cut and arranged into the decorated wooden sleighs. "And I don't need to guess what you're up to here. That sweet aroma of sugar and cinnamon is the telltale sign of glazed cinnamon nuts in progress."

"You know it!" Betty said. "As many as I can crank out this year. Sally's coming by in a bit to help fill the bags." Her eyes indicated a basket beside the baking sheets.

Mist followed Betty's gaze, noting the petite cellophane bags and gold ribbon waiting to be made into small gifts of the sweet, glazed nuts. A few were already filled, prototypes for the rest to match.

"These will be perfect for the hotel's sleigh ride gift, don't you think?" Betty looked at the ready examples and then at Mist, eyebrows raised.

"Perfect," Mist said. "Just enough to be a treat people can collect with the others they'll pick up along the way."

"I love the way this activity has developed," Betty said. "Sort of like trick-or-treating but at Christmastime. Did I tell you Millie plans to dress up as an old-time caroler?"

Mist brought her hands together in what might be interpreted as a silent clap or expression of appreciation. "How wonderful! What a great idea." She could picture it now, the vintage-style cape and cap lit up by the soft lighting Clayton planned to provide each booth. There had been some slight disappointment at not being able to use the old-fashioned kerosene lanterns that had been proposed, but Clayton, being the fire chief, vetoed that suggestion, replacing it with battery-powered options.

"Marge is wearing something similar," Betty continued. "And Sally might be dressing up as Mrs. Claus. I offered her an outfit I wore a few years ago for that Yuletide Festival, but she had already pulled something together from things in her thrift shop."

"I love the way this activity has continued to be embellished as townsfolk add their own ideas," Mist said. "It's become a true community activity."

"That's Timberton for you," Betty said. "People come together."

"Yes, they do." Mist smiled as she crossed to the sink and filled a pitcher with water that she'd use to fill the flower centerpieces. This was one thing she loved about the town, the way the residents came together as a community. Certainly there were those who kept to themselves. But many stepped forward to participate in town events.

"I'm going to put the centerpieces together out in the café

and then touch up the guest rooms a bit." Betty and Mist exchanged smiles. It was well known that these were two of Mist's favorite tasks. Setting up the centerpieces just before guests arrived allowed them to stay fresh for the Christmas Eve dinner. And choosing trinkets to place in the rooms seemed appropriate to not do too far in advance, as if the intuition of what to place in each room might be more keen closer to the guests' arrivals.

Mist took the water pitcher into the café and returned to the kitchen for the flowers. As she exited, she crossed paths with Sally, who was coming in to help Betty put the cellophane packages together.

"I heard a rumor Mrs. Claus might make an appearance on the sleigh route," Mist said by way of a greeting.

"Beautiful flowers!" Sally exclaimed. "And yes, the rumor is probably true. I'm still looking for something white to use as a trim. But I have the red outfit together."

Mist set the flowers down and searched her memory. "I might be able to help. I'll catch up to you in the kitchen."

It was always somewhat of a mystery what might be found in Mist's assortment of miscellaneous items she'd gathered over time. Kept in a back hall closet, the collection continued to grow. It now filled every shelf in the closet as well as bins and baskets on the floor. Wall hooks held even more, which is where Mist found what she'd hoped to find dangling from one of the hooks. She grabbed the item and took it to the kitchen.

"Oh my!" Sally exclaimed. "A white feather boa! How on earth?"

Betty laughed. "She has lost continents in that closet, Sally. Hundreds of knickknacks. Possibly thousands at this point."

Mist grinned. Betty was correct. She had, in fact, amused herself earlier in the year by attempting to count the trinkets.

She'd given up about halfway through when she reached six hundred.

"That should work," Mist said to Sally. "It's a little fluffy, but it will get the message across. Just cut it to whatever lengths you need."

"I hate to ruin it," Sally said.

"I assure you I don't need it." Mist laughed. "As Betty said, I have quite a few things in that closet."

"*Quite* a few things," Betty whispered to Sally.

Mist left Betty and Sally to their project and returned to the café, pleased that her closet of whimsical items had come in handy. She turned her attention to filling the miniature wooden sleighs with petite red roses, baby's breath, red berries, and greenery, snipping stems and inserting them in glass containers hidden inside the sleighs. To each she added an ivory orchid as a final touch before filling the inner glass with water and distributing them to tables. She then filled one larger sleigh with a similar but heartier arrangement and placed it in the center of the buffet.

After cleaning up the table she'd used for cutting and assembling the centerpieces, she moved on to the closet that had so graciously provided the answer to Sally's costuming needs. Here she curled up on the floor, her skirt settling over sturdy work boots, her favorite footwear in spite of its contrast to her typical bohemian style of dress. People were known to comment about the unusual way she could almost glide across a floor silently while wearing such heavy footwear.

Surveying the closet's contents was an activity Mist enjoyed with a certain reverence that one would not expect while sitting on the floor of a closet. But she'd found over the years that quietly contemplating the items led her to focus on certain ones as if they were reaching out to her, eager to become part of this year's guest experience. And so she picked out the ones that called to her: a silver beveled heart suncatcher, a vintage toy train engine, a trio of crocheted woodland animals, a blue floral teapot with mismatched cups, a ceramic bowl of sea glass, and a hand-painted wooden box with a brass hinge.

Mist stood and gathered the items together, adding a jigsaw puzzle at the last minute that would be perfect for the front parlor. Satisfied with her choices, she closed the closet and headed out to distribute them.

Chapter Four

M**IST HAD JUST FINISHED A TOUR OF THE HOTEL, DOUBLE**-checking rooms and common areas when the sound of the front door signaled the arrival of guests. Having ended up in the café, she placed the floral sleigh centerpiece she'd been admiring back on a table and headed to the lobby.

"Welcome to the Timberton Hotel," Mist said as she greeted the woman and two young girls. All sported colorful coats, winter boots, and gloves or mittens, and they all looked eager for a snowy holiday, as indicated by cheerful smiles and rosy cheeks. "You must be the Porter family."

"Indeed we are," the mother said. "I'm Ivy..." She then beckoned the girls back to her—they had been understandably drawn to the Christmas tree—and added, "and these are my girls, Sage and Sienna." She indicated the youngest and oldest in that order.

Mist bent over just slightly to address the girls specifically. She estimated their ages to be perhaps six and eight. "We're so glad you're here. You look like the kind of girls who might like

19

hot chocolate. Am I correct? I could be wrong, of course. Maybe you only like to drink water?"

Both girls giggled, and the older of the two spoke up. "We love hot chocolate, of course."

"Well!" Mist exclaimed. "That's a good thing. We just happen to have hot chocolate here at this hotel!"

"Every day?" Sage asked.

"Every day!"

Mist straightened up to address the mother and was suddenly taken by the sensation that the woman looked familiar. It was not entirely impossible that they'd met before, as they were both from Santa Cruz. But the beach city—in spite of feeling more like a town—was a city of sixty thousand people, and Mist had been gone for over a decade.

"We're delighted to have you with us for the Christmas holidays. My name is Mist, and I'll be happy to help you with anything you need. Our hotelkeeper, Betty, is always available too."

Ivy, listening quietly so far, now smiled and spoke up. "You're from Santa Cruz aren't you?"

"Yes, I am. I went to school there," Mist said, now knowing her instincts were correct. She and the woman had crossed paths before.

"I know you," Ivy said. "What an amazing coincidence to come to this little mountain town and run into you here."

"Indeed!" Mist tried to place the person from her past. A young teacher maybe? It was possible, though Mist didn't recognize the name Porter. Perhaps she'd married since then. The girls were young, but the woman appeared to be in her late thirties, so it was not out of the question if she'd started teaching when she was young. "Do you teach at UC Santa Cruz? Or did you at some point? I went to school there."

Ivy nodded. "I do, but I don't think I had you in one of my classes. I know you from the little café you worked at."

"Oh! Of course!" Suddenly Mist could picture her. Even after all the years, the image of a younger Ivy at a corner café table with a mug of herbal tea came back to her. Ivy had come into the café to read or write in a journal. She was often one of the last to leave. "You always sat at the same table. I can picture you there now with your tea and books and journal."

"It was my favorite place to be," Ivy said. "I could relax there, step away from academics. I knew I was welcome."

"And now you are welcome here at *this* café." Mist indicated the Moonglow Café off to the side of the foyer. "And the hotel, of course. We're delighted to have you here, all of you." She made a point of looking at each girl so they would know they were included.

"Look! They have sleigh rides!" Sienna pointed to a festive sign on the front desk. "Can we go?" She looked back and forth between her mother and Mist, not entirely sure who to ask.

"Oh, you must!" Mist said, directing her response to Ivy. "It's a special event this year, and it's going to be wonderful. It's not just any sleigh ride; it's an enchanted ride through the forest with surprise stops along the way."

"It sounds wonderful!" Ivy said. "We wouldn't miss it. Right, girls?"

"Right!" they both answered.

"Why don't we get you settled in your room, which is an upstairs suite that will be perfect for you and the girls."

Ivy turned to her daughters. "What do you think? Should we go see our room now?" Both girls nodded enthusiastically.

Mist placed a registration card and room key on the counter along with a pen. Ivy quickly filled out the form.

"We'll be serving dinner in the café in about an hour," Mist said. "Hotel guests are always welcome. It's included with your stay here. You'll see some of the local residents there too. The front parlor is a great place to relax." She indicated the archway to the room. "We keep a fire going most of the time, and there's a wonderful bookshelf with plenty of books. Plus we have a crafts table in the back."

"I love crafts," Sienna said.

"Me too!" Sage exclaimed, not to be left out.

"The beverage area here in the lobby is stocked with coffee, tea, hot chocolate, and often hot mulled cider," Mist continued. "You'll find treats there as well as these glazed cinnamon nuts here on the registration desk and in the front parlor." She slid a dish of the sweet nuts forward, and Ivy offered one to each of her daughters— "Just one, girls!"—and then tasted one herself.

"Delicious!" Ivy exclaimed. "Do you make these?"

"Betty does," Mist said. "It's a tradition of hers, a family recipe. She makes them every year. We can send the recipe home with you if you'd like."

"That would be wonderful," Ivy said as she helped herself to another one.

Mist escorted the trio upstairs to their suite, and the two women agreed to catch up later. Returning downstairs, Mist was charmed by the coincidence of having a hotel guest that she'd met in what seemed like another lifetime. It served as a reminder that life could be unpredictable. Which suited her just fine.

"Our first guests have arrived," Mist said as she joined Betty in the kitchen. "Ivy Porter and her two daughters, who are both adorable."

"They're the ones from Santa Cruz, right? Where you went to school?"

Mist nodded as she removed a large covered bowl of mixed greens from the refrigerator, removed its plastic cover, and proceeded to sprinkle golden raisins and sliced almonds on top of it. "Yes, and it turns out I do know her. Or at least recognize her."

"Really!" Betty exclaimed. "It's a small world, isn't it?"

"Yes, it is." Mist covered the salad again and placed it back in the refrigerator. "She used to come into the café where I worked. Always sat at the same table, was always very kind and appreciative. The perfect customer."

"Those girls are going to love the sleigh ride."

Mist laughed. "Yes, they're very excited about it. They also seemed excited about the craft table in the front parlor. Maybe I'll spruce it up a bit. I have some art supplies that aren't out there yet."

"Whatever you put out, they'll enjoy it," Betty said enthusiastically. "It's a great way for kids to pass the time. They won't want to sit around the fire listening to the adults talk for hours as tends to happen in there."

"Kids of all ages," Mist clarified. "You never know who might choose to pass the time at that table. We all have a bit of creative spirit inside us."

"You really think so? I'm not sure I do," Betty said. "Take art, for example. I can barely draw a stick figure."

"Maybe, but you knit," Mist pointed out. "You made a wonderful scarf for Marge's birthday this year. There are many ways to be creative. Someone might even create a sense of hope for someone through conversation. Words can be magical at times."

Betty nodded. "Yes, I see what you mean. And speaking of Marge and creating, I think I'll go create a little business for her by restocking my caramel stash."

Mist laughed. "Now you're getting the idea."

As Betty donned her winter coat and left for Marge's candy shop, Mist knew the short conversation itself had brought about an awareness. And that in itself was both creative and magical.

Chapter Five

Mist and Betty had just finished setting up a buffet of lasagna, mixed green salad, steamed broccoli, and garlic bread when the front door opened, and Clara and Andrew entered.

"Just in time for food!" Clive quipped. He set down a tray of brownies on the beverage table and extended a handshake to Andrew, who accepted and returned the gesture.

"I knew we timed our arrival right." Andrew turned to Clara. "Didn't I?"

"Yes, you did, dear," Clara said. She removed her gloves and cap and set them on the registration desk. Andrew helped her with her coat and then took his own off as Betty joined them. She and Clara exchanged hugs.

"You look ready for a good meal." Betty nodded at the buffet. "Do you want to dive right in or get settled into your room first?"

"Same room as always?" Clara asked.

"Of course," Betty said. "We know you love that room." She

and Mist made a point of putting returning guests in their favorite rooms. It was all a part of making them feel at home.

Clara looked at Andrew. "Let's take our things upstairs quickly and then come right back down."

"An excellent plan," Andrew agreed. He and Clive grabbed the suitcases and quickly deposited them in the second-floor guest room. Within minutes, they were all back downstairs. Clive attended to the fire in the front parlor, and Clara and Andrew helped themselves to the offerings at the buffet. Once they filled their plates, they took seats at a large table where Ivy and the girls already sat with their dinners.

"You've been here before, I take it," Ivy said after introducing herself and the girls.

"Oh, yes!" Clara exclaimed. "There's no place we'd rather be for Christmas. Andrew and I have been coming here for years. And I came before I was fortunate enough to meet this lovely man." She looked at Andrew with affection. She'd loved Timberton back before her first husband passed away. The two spent many holidays at the hotel. She'd even spent Christmas at the hotel on her own after that. Meeting Andrew and sharing it with him now reminded her how lucky she was, how it was possible to find happiness again.

With the buffet full and guests accommodated, Betty and Mist looked over the registration book in the kitchen while waiting for more garlic bread to come out of the oven.

Mist tapped her finger on a list of names. "Diana and Graham Hudson won't be able to make it tomorrow as planned. Their flight has been canceled due to bad weather."

"They're the ones coming from New York, right?" Betty opened the oven door, grabbed a hot pad, and pulled out a tray as Mist nodded in answer to her question. The aroma of garlic floated through the kitchen. She inhaled and then sighed. "I love the smell of garlic."

"And butter," Mist pointed out.

"Yes, and butter."

"And fresh baked bread…"

"Yes, yes." Betty laughed as she placed the garlic bread in baskets. "All of that. So will those guests have to cancel? The ones from New York?"

"No, fortunately," Mist said as she made a note in the book. "They found a flight the next day when the weather is expected to clear up. They just won't make it in tomorrow. They'll arrive the following day."

"Hopefully early enough in the day to take a sleigh ride," Betty said as she took a basket of bread in each hand. "They start that day."

Mist looked up and smiled. She'd been enchanted with the sleigh ride idea right from the start. She could hardly wait to see visitors and townsfolk enjoy the horse-drawn excursion through the winter landscape.

"There will be sleigh rides for three days," Mist said, grateful that two additional days had been added once enthusiasm for the activity grew. "So they'll have plenty of chances."

"Good point," Betty said. She passed through the door to the café to restock the garlic bread on the buffet, returning shortly.

"Your annual cookie exchange is that day too," Mist reminded Betty. "It'll be a busy day."

Betty nodded. "Downright hectic, I imagine."

"Just delightfully full of holiday activity," Mist said.

"Hectic," Betty said.

"Wonderfully rich with seasonal cheer."

Betty leaned forward and whispered, "Hectic."

"Brimming with merry festivities."

Betty soundlessly mouthed the word *hectic*.

"Replete with the spirit of Yuletide joy."

A new voice entered the conversation. "Okay, where is it?"

Mist and Betty both looked up, delighted to see the professor enter the kitchen. He looked around with a mock investigative air. Holding the teapot from his guest room—Mist always made sure he had one—he looked not unlike a detective bearing the proverbial magnifying glass.

"Where is what?" Betty asked as she watched him survey the counter.

"The thesaurus, my dear ladies. I have been listening to your intriguing conversation as I approached."

Mist and Betty exchanged amused looks.

"We're just discussing what a full day the twenty-third will be," Betty explained. "Breakfast, the cookie exchange, late guest arrivals, the sleigh rides starting, and dinner, of course."

"Brimming with brilliant jollification," the professor pronounced.

Betty picked up a soft, quilted hot pad off the counter and tossed it at the beloved British guest. She then quickly brought both hands to her mouth, eyes wide, having surprised even herself.

"You did not just do that!" the professor exclaimed after the lightweight fabric bounced off his shoulder and landed precariously on top of the teapot.

Mist's eyes grew as wide as Betty's. "I believe she did."

"And with a jolly good aim too!"

"Thank you, Professor!" Betty beamed, and all three broke into laughter just as Clive walked in.

"What did I miss?" Clive looked from one grinning face to another.

"Betty is throwing things at the professor," Mist said.

Clive looked at Betty, eyebrows raised.

"A bit of an exaggeration," the professor said in Betty's defense. "One wayward projectile, nothing I can't handle. Still, if I might get a spot of hot water for tea, I shall take my leave before things escalate."

Mist took the teapot—retrieving the hot pad at the same time—and filled it with boiling water, cautioning the professor to wait for it to cool slightly before drinking it.

"Thank you, my dear Mist. Every precaution will be taken." The professor nodded and took his leave.

Mist and Betty exchanged looks of amusement and then stepped through the kitchen's swinging door and back into the café.

"It sounded like quite a party in there," Michael said, grinning. "I thought about coming to the rescue, but I knew Nigel could hold his own." Rain, sitting next to him in a high chair, saw Mist approaching and raised her arms to be held. Mist lifted her from the chair, got her settled on her hip, and then poked her nose with a finger, causing her to giggle.

"Hello, sweet girl," Mist said. "Would you like to come with me to see how our guests are enjoying their meals?" Jiggling Rain up and down playfully, Mist made the rounds of the room, content to see conversations and laughter. She joined in briefly at several tables and then stood back, watching the room with satisfaction. Because mealtimes were never just about meals in the Moonglow Café. They provided a chance to share stories and get to know each other, just as she intended.

Chapter Six

"Waffles!" Sage squealed when she caught sight of the breakfast offerings the following morning. Sienna backed her up with a sisterly fist pump to signal her approval.

"These are blueberry pecan waffles," Mist pointed out, "but we have plain ones, too, if you prefer." She greeted Ivy, who trailed just behind the girls, with a smile.

"Plain for me, please," Sage said.

"I'm going for blueberry pecan!" Sienna declared. "I'm an adventurer!"

"Sienna loves trying new things," Ivy said. "Sage is a little more cautious, which is just fine." She patted her younger daughter's shoulder.

"Absolutely fine," Mist said. "Why, some days I want something plain while other days I want something fancy."

"Really?" Sage asked.

"Yes, really," Mist said. "You'll always have choices here."

Ivy smiled. "Then I'll choose some of that lovely fruit." She indicated a bowl near the chafing dish of waffles. "So festive with the green and red!"

"Wait," Sienna said. "I can tell you what's in it... strawberries, honeydew melon, kiwi, and red and green grapes. Christmas colors! Oh, and some kind of little red something-or-others."

"Pomegranate seeds," Mist said, stepping back as she saw others entering the café. "Help yourselves. You'll find a warming tray of bacon, some gingerbread muffins, and fresh orange juice as you follow the buffet."

"Good morning!" Clara said as she and Andrew stepped into the café. "What a delight it is to wake up here!"

"I agree," Andrew said. "The first morning here always feels special, sort of like waking up from a dream and then finding yourself in one."

"That's a good way to put it," Clara said.

The sound of the front door opening and closing signaled the arrival of a local, and William Guthrie—known to all as Wild Bill—appeared in the café's doorway. "Something smells good!" he proclaimed.

"Have a seat, Bill," Clive said, tapping him on the shoulder as he stepped around him. "You're blocking the door." The lighthearted teasing served its purpose. The owner of the greasy spoon appropriately called Wild Bill's took a seat at a table near the buffet, where Clayton and his fire crew—often first in line for meals—already sat. It was not uncommon for Wild Bill to show up for breakfast, his little café a few miles outside of town having evolved—or one might say devolved—into rarely being open. Instead, it had taken to offering special events every so often that were wildly popular. One such event, the Burnt Toast Extravaganza, drew over one hundred people, and his Some Facsimile of a Pancake Breakfast drew even more. Undoubtedly, much of this had to do with Sally of Second Hand Sally's thrift shop, now his partner, overseeing the kitchen during those events.

Mist was especially delighted to see Hollister arrive. The formerly homeless man who lived downstairs in the hotel had recently started joining others for meals after many years of not doing so. Both deaf and mute, the locals and yearly hotel regulars knew him and communicated as well as possible. It was proof that smiles and handshakes and expressions could go a long way. Additionally helpful was the fact Mist had become quite adept at sign language, something she'd made an effort to learn after realizing Hollister understood it.

Wherever Hollister went, a trusty sidekick accompanied him. This explained the ball of fur who slipped quietly under the table as if he knew sneaking into a café was the only way to pull it off. The rescue dog had an affinity for bacon, so much so that it became his name. This also explained his current fascination with the buffet. Bacon was smelling the bacon.

"Any plans for today?" Clive asked, directing his question to no one in particular. "I'm planning to chop some wood." One of his tasks was keeping the fireplace in the front parlor going.

"While that sounds really exciting, Clive," Clara said to laughter around the room, "I plan to do some shopping. I hear Duffy's has a great gift section this year, and Marge's candy shop is always calling my name."

"Yes, go to Duffy's," Ivy said. "We went down there yesterday after we checked in. The selection of items in the gifts is fantastic, especially the local products."

"And they have ice-cream sodas," Sienna added.

"Strawberry," Sage said.

"And other flavors," Sienna pointed out.

"Yes." Ivy grinned. "Many other flavors. But do look at the gifts. I saw a wonderful stained glass suncatcher that I might go back for. It's small enough to be a Christmas ornament, but it would look wonderful hanging in the kitchen window. There are quite a few there, most of them mountain scenes. The designs are very soothing."

"I'll check those out for sure," Clara said. "I've always loved stained glass. I also want to stop by the gallery to see what Clive has designed lately. I'm thinking to give one of his charms to a friend from church."

Ivy perked up. "Charms? I have a charm bracelet that I've had for years. I'm always looking for something to add."

"We have charm bracelets too," Sienna said. Sage nodded, her mouth full of blueberry waffle.

"Yes, you do," Ivy said, smiling. "Your grandmother gave you those."

"I'll be there as soon as I finish with the wood," Clive said. "Addison's fantastic with the customers, but I don't want her to get overwhelmed if it gets crowded."

"And people like to meet the designer when they buy custom jewelry." Mist pointed this out as she brought out a serving dish of hot waffles to add to the buffet. Betty followed just behind with a new batch of bacon, one slice of which "accidentally" fell on the floor as she passed by Hollister's table.

"I suppose that's true," Clive said. "And I enjoy telling them about the process as well as the history of sapphire mining in this area. Which means I'd better get going." He grabbed a waffle from the new batch as if it were a muffin—granted, it was sticking off the plate, so he didn't touch any others—and headed out, passing the professor as he entered.

"How is everyone on this lovely morning?"

Andrew responded first. "Excellent. Just fortifying myself to beat you in a chess game."

"I shall look forward to proving you wrong," the professor quipped as he helped himself to a waffle and fruit at the buffet and took a seat. Mist soon slid a teapot of hot water next to him along with his favorite PG Tips tea.

And so the morning went, with people coming and going, seeking coffee, breakfast, company, or all three. Mist retired to the kitchen once the breakfast crowd slowly disbursed.

Michael brought Rain by, settling her in the kitchen's high chair so he could help with cleanup so it wouldn't all fall on Betty and Mist. Taking advantage of the welcome help, Mist decided to run to Duffy's for fresh herbs to use for that evening's dinner. She kissed both husband and daughter and slipped out the back door.

Chapter Seven

Mist grinned as she walked into Duffy's. The classic "Grandma Got Run Over by a Reindeer" played on the shop's sound system. Duffy had an understated sense of humor, and the playlist he'd created for holiday shoppers showed it. She'd heard the selections already when she'd stopped in a few days before, so she knew "I Saw Mommy Kissing Santa Claus" and "All I Want for Christmas"—an ode to missing teeth—would be following.

"What can I do for you on this lovely, fine day?" Duffy said. He seemed exceptionally chipper, something many had noticed recently. Rumor had it that a bit of romance might have popped up in his life, though no one knew for sure. No one was going to ask the typically quiet man about anything personal. Others said it was a result of business being good, which was certainly the case. Duffy's had become an integral part of the community, so much so that it was hard to imagine that it was ever not there. Whatever the case, it was delightful to see him so happy.

"I'm just here to pick up some fresh tarragon," Mist replied as she aimed for the selection of fresh herbs that Duffy kept in the produce area. It was undoubtedly her favorite section of the store. Just seeing the various herbs inspired ideas for meals. There was nothing like fresh oregano, thyme, or dill to make seasonings just right. "And maybe some sage," she added, picking out a little of each.

As Mist debated additional herbs, a woman approached a barrel of carrots—Duffy always merchandised products creatively—and began to fill a basket. Two carrots became four became eight became twenty in no time at all.

"I love carrots," Mist said by way of casual conversation. "Often with a bit of tarragon and honey." She held up the herbs.

"That sounds delicious," the woman said, smiling. "But my crew isn't very fussy. They'll eat them any old way, preferably whole. I can never have enough carrots around. I buy them by the twenty-five-pound bag at home."

"Is that so?" It didn't take long for Mist to connect the dots, or carrots, so to speak. "Might your crew be of the equine variety?"

"How did you guess?"

"I'm Mist. We spoke on the phone." Mist offered a handshake, surprised as the woman's smooth, flawless hand slid into her own. It made Mist question what she had expected, perhaps rough hands from working outdoors or handling the horses' reins. It was a reminder that having preconceived notions was often a fool's pastime.

Christine returned the handshake with a warm smile. "Oh! From the hotel! How wonderful. I was just on my way over there. It's right down the street, isn't it?"

"Yes, very close." Mist added some oregano to her other choices. "I'll walk there with you, if you'd like."

"I'd like that very much," Christine said. "I'll just purchase these snacks for Chester and Missy."

Mist followed her to the register. After both women finished their purchases—amid some small-town banter with Duffy—they headed for the hotel.

Christine Hubbard was nothing like Mist had pictured her to be. She was a waif of a woman, barely one hundred pounds in Mist's estimation, with wavy blond hair that reached her waist even when held back with a barrette. Her light blue eyes were large enough to seem out of proportion in her slender face, and her skin resembled porcelain, without a single blemish or wrinkle. She reminded Mist of a doll. She had a sudden urge— which she would wisely ignore—to call her Chrissy.

"Welcome to the Timberton Hotel, Christine." Mist offered the official greeting as they entered the hotel.

"Please, just call me Chris. I'm delighted to be here!" The woman glanced around the lobby and peeked into the front parlor. "How charming! The decorations are lovely, and your Christmas tree is beautiful. This certainly beats sleeping in the barn." She laughed in such a way as to make Mist question if she was kidding or not.

"Surely you wouldn't expect to sleep there?" The question slipped out of Mist's mouth unexpectedly.

Christine laughed. "Oh, it's been known to happen before. And it's not as bad as it sounds. It's rather lovely to be near the horses. They're family to me."

"I understand," Mist said. "Just as pets are family to people."

"Yes, exactly."

Mist took a key from the wall rack and handed it to Christine along with a registration card to sign. "Your room is ready for you. It's actually right down the hall here." She gestured to a hallway between the registration desk and the café. Although most of the guest rooms were upstairs, there was one always ready on the first floor for situations where a guest needed to avoid stairs or, in this case, when the hotel was at maximum capacity.

Betty emerged from the kitchen, passing through the café and joining them in the lobby. "Here you are, the woman with the horses! Christine, right?"

"Yes, that would be me. And just Chris is fine."

"I detect a slight accent, don't I?" Betty noted.

Christine smiled. "Guilty as charged. I grew up in Kentucky, though I've been in Montana for about five years."

"I want to hear all about the horses," Betty said. "I grew up around horses."

Mist looked at Betty with surprise. "I never knew that."

"Oh yes," Betty said. "I can tell you tales from my youth."

"I'd love to hear them," Christine said.

"So would I!" Mist said to Betty before turning back to Christine. "You'll get a chance to hear all kinds of stories later. People usually relax in the front parlor after dinner for just that reason: sharing stories."

"It's a plan." Christine smiled. "I have a few to tell myself."

"I imagine you do!" Betty exclaimed. "I look forward to hearing them." She turned to Mist and picked up the fresh herbs from the counter where Mist had set them. "Why don't I take these to the kitchen?" Receiving a nod of thanks from Mist, she excused herself.

"Let me show you to your room. You can settle in and relax." Mist led Christine down the hallway and left her to get situated. She then returned to the kitchen to find Betty putting on her coat.

"You're full of surprises, Betty."

The hotelkeeper laughed. "Aren't we all?"

"I believe you're right," Mist said, knowing we rarely knew everything there was to know about a person, even after many years.

Betty buttoned her coat and grabbed her gloves and knit cap. "I'm going down to the gallery to help Addison. I'm sure it's busy with Christmas shoppers, and Clive's over at Duffy's touching up the sleigh."

"Addison will appreciate the help, I'm sure."

"And speaking of help," Betty continued, "Maisie said she'd be here later, after she closes the flower shop, to help in the kitchen."

"Wonderful."

Mist knew she received the credit for the meals that were served in the Moonglow Café. But the truth was that they were often a group effort, Maisie being the biggest helper of all. In fact, this was one of the many things that made the town of Timberton special, people's willingness to help each other.

Chapter Eight

A CRACKLING FIRE SET THE COZY BACKDROP IN THE FRONT parlor as guests settled in after a hearty dinner of tarragon chicken, vegetarian stuffed acorn squash, and roasted fingerling potatoes, followed by apple crisp for those who still had room for dessert.

Sage and Sienna had headed for the craft table as soon as they entered the room, where they found magazines and scissors for making collages and also a tray of jewelry-making supplies. Sienna grabbed a small poster board and started contemplating pictures while Sage selected colorful beads for a necklace.

"I need to get out and see more of this town," Ivy said as she stood by the fire, enjoying the warmth. "Maybe even a night stroll to see all the lights."

"We take walks here just about every day," Clara said as she and Andrew eased into places on the sofa. "It's wonderful as long as you bundle up in warm outerwear. All the shops have amazing holiday displays in the windows, and the Christmas tree in the town park lights up as it begins to get dark. Duffy runs a train around the display in his front window."

"Not just any train," the professor noted. "It's a prewar Lionel O gauge set with a 1688 engine. His father owned it as a child, gave it to Duffy on his sixth birthday."

"I'm not sure what that means, but it sounds impressive," Clara said.

"It's probably just that accent," Andrew said. "Everything sounds impressive with a British accent."

The professor, choosing to take the high road, said nothing.

"And Marge always has samples to enjoy in her candy shop," Andrew added. "Though I guess that might counteract the point of taking the walk."

Michael, relaxing with Rain on his lap in his favorite chair near the fireplace, spoke up. "I want to hear about your trip this past summer."

"You mean the one where we had to put up with the professor?" Andrew sent a comical look to the person in question, who sat across from Michael.

"He's just kidding, of course!" Clara playfully smacked Andrew's arm. "Nigel was the perfect host and tour guide. And staying with his sister Chloe and niece Poppy was delightful!"

"Do they live in London?" Betty asked as she refilled a crystal bowl of glazed cinnamon nuts. "That's where you're from originally, isn't it, Professor?"

"Indeed it is," the professor replied. "I acquired my impressive accent there." He shot Andrew a look that faintly resembled a smirk. "But my sister is out in the Cotswolds. She's lived there for many years, though we grew up in London."

"Oh, it was so lovely!" Clara exclaimed. "It was everything I ever imagined the English countryside would be. We did go into London for a day to see sights like Westminster Abbey, Big Ben, and the Tower of London. And we had a fabulous afternoon tea at the Goring Hotel. But most of our time was spent in the Cotswolds. It was simply enchanting!"

The professor beamed with a look of pride as if he had personally created the English countryside. "I've always loved Chloe's cottage," he said. "It's not large, but it's quite splendid."

"Yes, it is," Clara said. "Like something out of a storybook: stone walls, pitched roof, beautiful garden with brick walkways and trimmed hedges and all types of flowers. And the living room was delightful with its exposed beams and big fireplace."

"Limestone and brick, that fireplace," Andrew added.

"Yes," the professor said. "That's very traditional. The cottage itself is built with limestone from the Jurassic era. You'll see it all over the countryside. It's often called Cotswold stone. Quite beautiful, typically a honey color."

"No dinosaurs?" Sienna asked, having caught the word *Jurassic*.

"Not a one," the professor said.

"Nigel took us all over," Clara continued, "even to Oxford."

"Your alma mater, I believe," Michael said. "Isn't that right?"

The professor nodded. "Quite correct."

"That was fascinating," Andrew said, leaning forward. "The architecture alone is worth a visit. The Bodleian Library —which should really be plural because it's composed of twenty-eight libraries—and the Radcliffe Camera were both phenomenal."

"We saw some of the places *Harry Potter* was filmed." Clara raised her voice intentionally to get Sage and Sienna's attention, and it worked.

"You did?" Both girls left the craft area and joined the others.

"Yes, we did," Clara said. "New Library and Christ

Church both have locations used in the films as well as other places we saw."

"That's so cool," Sienna said. "I love *Harry Potter*."

"Me too," Sage exclaimed. "Especially the staircases! Did you see those?"

Clara nodded. "Yes, we did. Those are in Christ Church."

Sara hopped from one foot to the other eagerly. "Did they move?"

"Not while we were there," Clara said, grinning.

"I suspect that only happens in the films, my dear girls," the professor said.

Having ascertained there were neither dinosaurs nor moving staircases in the stories being told, Sara and Sienna returned to the craft table, and the conversation continued.

"I took them to a pub or two," the professor said. "You cannot visit the UK without visiting traditional watering holes."

"Even if you have to beg for ice," Andrew noted.

The professor tutted. "I'll never understand the fascination you Americans have with ice." He looked at Andrew reprovingly. "But you *did* get ice after asking for it, so I wouldn't complain."

"Two ice cubes," Andrew clarified.

"All in all, it was an amazing trip," Clara said. "One we owe entirely to the professor for suggesting it last year."

"And what about this coming year?" Mist, who'd been listening to the discussion from the archway to the front lobby, asked.

Both Clara and Andrew shrugged. "No idea," Clara said. "We might even decide at the last minute, sometime this coming summer. Maybe a destination here in the US. There are so many places to see without leaving the country."

Christine entered the parlor and pulled a chair closer to the discussion. "Do I hear talk of US travel? I love taking road trips. You can see so many things you wouldn't see by flying."

"That's a good point," Clara said, turning to Andrew. "Maybe we should take a road trip, explore little towns along the way."

"Route 66 might be fun," Andrew suggested.

"Or Hwy 1 along the California coast," Christine said.

"You could go to New Orleans," Michael said.

"Ah, Cajun food and jazz," Andrew said. "That could be fun. I wouldn't mind some red beans and rice along with some great music on Bourbon Street."

"Then drive north along the Natchez Trace," Michael continued. "Lots of history and beautiful scenery."

"So many choices," Clara said. "I guess we'll just see where we end up. Wherever we go, I'm sure we'll have stories to tell here next year."

Christine turned toward Betty. "Speaking of stories to tell, you said you grew up around horses, didn't you?"

"You did?" Sage was back from the craft table in a flash. She looked at Betty eagerly. "How many did you have?"

Betty laughed. "I didn't have any of my own. But we lived in a rural area, and our neighbors on both sides had horses. I often hung out by the fence to feed them carrots."

Sage looked at Christine. "They like carrots, right?"

Christine nodded. "Yes, they love them."

"I want to feed your horses carrots," Sage said, her eyes bright. "Can I?"

"*May* I," Ivy whispered.

Sage sighed but accompanied it with a smile. "May I?"

"I bet we can arrange that if Betty and Mist have any spare carrots they don't need," Christine said.

"We just might have one, even two," Betty said. "I bet you and your sister would both like one."

Sienna called over from the craft table, having overheard the suggestion. "Count me in."

And with that, one of many plans for the next day had formed. It would be a double carrot day for the horses. In addition, the sleigh rides would begin, and Betty would hold her annual cookie exchange.

Knowing she was leaving the guests in the perfect company of each other, Mist retired to the back room where she kept her art supplies. She was already getting a feeling of being acquainted with this year's guests, at least those who'd already arrived. It was time to begin the traditional gifts they'd be given at the end of their visit. Setting miniature canvases into a custom frame that Clive had built her years ago, she chose colors that called to her, picked up a paintbrush, and began.

Chapter Nine

Mist set a stack of breakfast plates down in the kitchen, ready to be loaded into the dishwasher. Hearing voices, she wiped her hands on her vintage apron and headed out to the lobby, where she found a happy—though tired—couple waiting. Diana Hudson, a tall, slender woman with an oval face, removed a nubby knit cap to reveal short hair with wisps of silver. She slid out of her coat and draped it over her arm. Her husband, Graham, was slightly shorter with a stocky build. He set two suitcases down and pulled a strap off his shoulder, setting a camera bag down as well.

"You made it!" Mist said, pleased to see the Hudsons. "And earlier today than you thought. We were so sorry to hear your flight yesterday was canceled."

"Yes," Diana said. "But at least we were able to catch a late flight into Bozeman instead of waiting for the one we thought we'd have to take today. Which saved us from spending the night in the airport, thankfully."

"We got into Bozeman very late," Graham added. "So we

decided to spend the night there and drive here in the morning."

"A good thing," Diana said. "Your mountain roads are tricky in places."

Mist nodded. When asked about driving conditions by guests, she advised arriving in the light. It was safer in any case with the wildlife in the area. "Well, you're here now. We were just cleaning up from breakfast, but we have fruit and muffins I could bring out if you'd like."

"Thank you, but it's not necessary," Diana said. "We had something to eat before driving here. We'll be fine."

"Then let's get you settled in so you can enjoy the day." Mist took their room keys down from the wall rack while Diana filled out the registration card. She then gave a brief overview of the beverage bar, café, front parlor, and highlights of the town, including suggestions to visit Duffy's store and Clive's gallery. After showing them to their room, she returned to the kitchen, finding that Betty had finished loading the dishwasher.

"That was Diana and Graham Hudson," Mist said, knowing Betty would have heard the voices from the kitchen. "I'm so glad they made it here this early today."

"These are the ones whose flight was canceled, right?"

"Yes. They were going to take a flight today, but they managed to get one last night," Mist said. "I'm so pleased for them. At least they'll have one regular day to enjoy here instead of only being here for Christmas Eve and Christmas."

"And the sleigh rides start today," Betty pointed out.

"Yes, they do!" Mist could hardly contain her joy at the thought. So much preparation had gone into this event, and it was finally here.

"Have you seen the sleigh?" Betty smiled. "Clive and I went down to see it yesterday. It looks wonderful."

"I'm sure it does," Mist said. "I haven't seen it since they decorated it. Maybe I'll sneak down there today now that all the guests are checked in. It's parked behind Duffy's, right?"

"Yes, he and Clive moved it over there yesterday. It looked so funny being pulled by a pickup truck!" Betty chuckled. "It'll certainly be more appealing with the horses in front!"

Mist laughed, picturing the two scenarios. "You're right about that."

"Do I hear you two making fun of my truck?" Clive said, stepping into the kitchen. He gave Betty a peck on the cheek.

"Only casually," Betty said. "You know the horses will provide the right ambiance."

"I suppose so," Clive admitted. "Though you're missing out on being able to call it a 'one truck open sleigh.'" He sauntered over to a cookie jar and peeked inside, sighed, and replaced the lid.

Mist smiled. "The other cookie jar, Clive." She nodded to another counter where a large ceramic snowman sat.

Clive crossed the kitchen, pleased with what he found when he lifted the snowman's hat. "Ah, that's more like it!" He pulled a cookie out of the jar and took a bite.

"The rides start at three o'clock, right?" Betty asked.

"Yes, they run from three o'clock to eight o'clock," Mist said. "This gives people a chance to take it before it gets dark if they want."

"Oh!" Betty exclaimed. "That wouldn't be my choice. Not with all the twinkling lights and magical ambiance the evening hours promise. I've seen how much work Clive and Duffy have put into setting this up." She patted Clive on the shoulder.

"Duffy and I can't take all that credit," Clive said. "A lot of it goes to Millie, Sally, and Glenda. They've decorated every station and made sure each one has whatever it needs." He finished off the cookie, took another, and headed for the side door. "I'd better go give Duffy a hand. Chris is bringing the horses down from the barn now, and Duffy's store is mighty busy. They might need help bringing the sleigh around once the horses are hooked up."

Betty turned to Mist after Clive left. "I can hardly wait to see this. I'm so glad the sleigh rides start and end in front of the hotel."

Mist smiled. This had been debated for several days when the idea of the event first came up. In the end, it made the most sense to have the hotel be the location. In many ways—the Moonglow Café being not the least of those—the hotel was the center of town activity. It was where many had their meals, and it was the place locals knew they could "sneak in" for a free cup of coffee from the lobby or a fireside chat.

"The front parlor will give people a warm place to wait for rides," Mist said. "Though I suspect some will want to wait on the porch to watch."

"They might. Clive put heaters out there for that reason. And you have a table set up for coffee and hot chocolate. It's going to be wonderful!"

"You know what I think would be wonderful?" Mist said casually, knowing Betty was itching to see the horses. "If you went down to Duffy's to help get the sleigh ready to go." As Mist expected, Betty's face lit up.

"Well... I suppose they might need some extra help," Betty mused.

"Or Chris might need help with the horses," Mist added, knowing this wasn't likely, but it would be Betty's main motivation for going.

"I guess if you don't mind me leaving you alone for a bit."

Mist now fought back a grin as Betty had already taken a step toward the kitchen's coatrack. "Not at all! Everything is ready for the cookie exchange, and it doesn't start for a couple of hours." This was true. Michael had already moved the tables into the long row that was their standard setup for the event. All she needed to do was set out the cookie containers and do a quick check of the room.

"All right, you talked me into it!" Betty donned her coat, gloves, and knit cap, and slipped out the side door.

Mist fixed herself a cup of ginger-peach tea and sat down at the center island. Sometimes it wasn't too challenging to persuade someone to take a suggestion. As she took a sip of tea and thought of Betty getting to greet the horses, she was delighted this was one of those times.

Chapter Ten

THERE WERE FEW HOLIDAY ACTIVITIES AS BELOVED AT THE Timberton Hotel as Betty's annual cookie exchange. And it wasn't just the lure of sweet treats that made it special. It was the gathering of townsfolk for the tradition of sharing with each other. And what better thing to share than homemade sweets created with the expectation of making the holidays a little sweeter for others.

This was Betty's event, and Mist always chose to stand back and let Betty take the glory, knowing it was her time to shine. The annual cookie exchange had begun years before Mist arrived in Timberton. It was one event Betty could continue on her own. With one exception: Mist had offered—and Betty had readily accepted—her help with whatever containers would hold the cookies and other treats gathered into assortments.

The usual hunt for containers had turned out to be easy this year. Mist had spotted a small basket on a shelf in the gift section at Duffy's store that seemed to call out to her. She'd ordered several dozen from him and painted a winter scene on each. It hadn't been hard to decide what to paint. Nothing fit this season better than a sleigh surrounded by a winter forest scene accented with silver and gold touches. It would be a reminder of this particular year, something participants could save and reuse in the future.

Of all the holiday events, this was one that Betty dressed up for, always with a festive flair. And so, as Mist finished checking the table arrangement and placement of the baskets to be filled, she was surprised to see Betty step into the room in somewhat plain attire. Although the colors reflected the season —green skirt and red turtleneck—that was the extent of the outfit. No vest with holiday designs, no jewelry, not so much as a red or green hair clip. And to top it off, Betty had nothing on her feet but socks.

Cautiously choosing a polite comment, Mist spoke up. "Betty, you're not wearing shoes."

Betty grinned. "Don't worry, I will be. I have just the right ones."

"I'm a big fan of not wearing shoes, as you know." Mist thought back to her childhood, how she would take her shoes off every chance she had. Other than at work, she still was often barefoot.

"Yes, I know. I've seen you without them plenty of times in the back."

Mist smiled. It was true. Even at the hotel, if she wasn't working around food or with guests, she would take them off. As it happened, Rain tended to get fussy whenever Mist put shoes on her. Like mother, like daughter. And she absolutely wouldn't tolerate the toddler-sized pink cowboy boots that Clive had given her. The two of them had finally agreed—not that Clive had much choice—to keep them on a shelf in Rain's room as decoration. The fact she loved to point at them and say "boots!" then burst into giggles did help assuage Clive's feelings.

"I just wanted to get a peek at the room before everyone gets here," Betty said, looking around. "And of course it looks wonderful. I love all the sleigh centerpieces lined up down the middle of the table. Those flower arrangements look so festive together."

"Thank you," Mist said, stepping forward to straighten one of them slightly. Having the café tables in one long row for the event had allowed half the sleighs to face one direction down the center of the table while the other half faced the opposite direction. The baskets for participants to fill sat in the center.

"I'd better put my shoes on." Betty winked and headed out of the café, exiting through the kitchen door. Mist was both charmed and puzzled by Betty's behavior. A wink was out of character for her, leading Mist to conclude that she was up to some kind of mischief.

"And I'd better set the music." Mist headed for the sound system, which was controlled from a closet in the front parlor. Betty's countenance was intriguing, and Mist tumbled possible scenarios through her mind while choosing a cheerful playlist of upscale holiday classics. With the music set, she returned to the café to watch over things until Betty returned.

The first of the cookie bearers—or one could say treat-bearers as other sweets were included in the exchange if they could fit into an assortment—arrived before Betty returned. Mist, who normally would be stepping away at this point to let Betty take over, greeted Marge, who was often the first to arrive and rarely stayed more than a few minutes, as her candy shop was busy the last few days before Christmas. But she never missed the event, always showing up with something delightful. In this case, it was a tray of double chocolate fudge, cut into bite-sized squares, sure to be a crowd pleaser.

As Mist faced her and accepted the fudge to place on the table, Marge looked over her shoulder and gasped with delight. "Betty, look at you!" she exclaimed.

Mist turned and could hardly believe her eyes. Betty did indeed have shoes on—bright green elf shoes that curled up at the toes. But it was the rest of her outfit that proved Mist's instincts had been right in thinking Betty was up to something mischievous. Betty had turned into a festive Christmas tree thanks to a felt costume that stretched from pointy head to elf toes. Appliquéd ornaments dotted both the front and back of the clever costume. Only her face, arms, and elf shoes showed outside the costume.

"You see?" Betty quipped. "I put shoes on."

Mist laughed. "You certainly did. And a few branches too!"

"You look fabulous!" Marge exclaimed. Her enthusiasm was soon echoed by Sally and Glenda, who arrived bearing raspberry swirl cookies and peanut butter snowballs. They placed them on the table and fell into animated conversation with Betty, who understandably became the hit of the party. Very rarely did anything upstage the impressive buffet of sugary treats that the cookie exchange offered, but this year Betty appeared to have done just that.

"Between the cookie exchange and the sleigh rides starting, I can barely think straight!" Millie exclaimed as she slipped in and added a tray of peppermint bark to the table. "And Betty! Look at you!"

Little by little, the room grew busier, and the table grew sweeter as pumpkin chocolate chip cookies, carrot cake cookies, cherry bars, and other sweets joined the offerings. As participants each chose a colorfully decorated basket and began filling it with treats, Mist slipped out of the room, smiling as the cheerful sounds of joy mixed with upbeat Christmas music continued behind her. After all, this was always Betty's special event, and this year above all, there was no question of that.

Chapter Eleven

A CLATTER OF FOOTSTEPS ON THE HOTEL STAIRS WAS quickly followed with words of caution. "Slow down, girls!"

"We can't!" a young voice shouted. "We're too excited!"

Mist smiled, easily picturing the scene from the café where she was setting up the dinner buffet. She stepped into the lobby just in time to see Sage almost trip off the bottom step. She reached out to help, but the young girl managed to catch herself.

"I just don't want you to get hurt," Ivy said as she caught up with Sage and Sienna. "And we need to be respectful of other guests too."

"But we're horses, and this is our barn!" Sage said. She then burst into giggles at her own statement, which Sienna only acknowledged by rolling her eyes. "Just pretend, of course," Sage clarified once the giggles calmed down.

"You're going on the first sleigh ride, aren't you?" Mist asked. "Or at least one of the first."

Ivy nodded as she helped Sage put on a coat. "That's the plan. I think they go out every thirty minutes?"

"Approximately," Mist said. "That's our best guess based on the distance and number of stops along the way. The sleigh will go out again each time it returns, taking the next group waiting."

"It's going to stop?" Sienna asked. The expression on her face showed a dubious response to the idea.

"Oh yes," Mist said. "Wonderful stops. You'll see. And that's why you're going to take these with you." She lifted three miniature tote bags off a stack on the registration desk and handed one to each girl and then to Ivy.

"How adorable!" Ivy exclaimed, admiring the canvas handle bags with a simple evergreen tree on the front. Mist had painted the bags over several months after the suggestion of the sleigh ride became a reality. With plenty of time before the event, and a simple tree design involving only a dozen brush strokes, it had been easy to prepare enough. At least Mist hoped there would be enough. There were a good two hundred bags ready to go, and the sleigh ride had not been advertised outside Timberton, the intention being to keep it a community event. Still, tickets had been sold to cover the cost of the event with any extra proceeds going to the library's literacy program.

"Are you going?" Sage asked. "You should come. It's going to be so fun!"

Mist smiled, touched at the young girl's invitation. "Maybe later. I want to make sure food and beverages are ready, both in the café and on the front porch. Maybe you can tell me what it's like when you get back. How does that sound?"

"We'll give you a full report," Sienna said.

"Don't forget these!" Betty smiled as she handed each girl a carrot.

"Thank you!" Both girls grabbed the carrots eagerly and headed to the front door, their mother just behind.

Mist followed them and watched from the door as they

walked down the front walkway and offered the horses their treats. She then stepped out on the front porch, enchanted with the scene before her. As everyone had hoped, not plowing the road in front of the hotel for the previous two weeks had allowed enough snow to build up to let the sleigh ride begin right in front of the hotel. Customers had still been able to drive on side streets as well as the street running parallel behind shops. The slight inconvenience for shoppers had been well worth it. The decorated sleigh, fanciful horses—or were they reindeer considering the antlers on their heads?—and costumed driver—Christine as an adorable elf—looked like something out of a fairy tale.

Sage and Sienna shrieked with delight as Christine and Ivy helped them into their seats and spread blankets over their laps.

"Don't the horses ever get to ride?" Sage asked.

Sienna laughed. "That would be funny but not possible."

"They don't," Christine said. "But they love taking people out on rides."

Graham, standing on the sidewalk, snapped a few photos of the enthusiastic scene. Several others joined the group, and then, with a cheerful jingling of sleigh bells, they were off and away.

Mist greeted others who were arriving to take one of the next rides out, pleased to see that Diana and Graham were among them. She indicated the hot chocolate service on the porch and also invited them to come inside if they wished. Excusing herself, she returned to the café and kitchen, where she found Betty and Maisie prepping the casual dinner buffet that had been chosen for that night.

"This looks perfect," Mist said as she surveyed the trays of sandwich makings. Knowing the afternoon and evening would be busy with sleigh rides, she'd decided on an easy meal to feed everyone: soup and make-your-own sandwiches. Opening the café earlier than usual and keeping the closing time flexible, people could stop in and grab something to eat just before or after their ride. Not that a simple meal with Mist was exactly like any simple meal. Bread choices ranged from ciabatta rolls to honey-wheat bread to buttery croissants. Sandwich fixings numbered in the dozens. And three large cauldrons of soup offered options of hearty minestrone, creamy carrot-ginger, and good old chicken noodle. And not to leave out dessert, a tray of white chocolate cranberry cookies rested at the end of the buffet.

"This is your idea of simple..." a voice nearby mused. Mist turned to see the professor surveying the abundant spread.

"It is indeed," Mist replied. "There's no cooking—the soups were already made and just needed to be heated up—no need to set the tables, and only easy replenishing of the buffet is needed. So almost no preparation."

"And the biscuits?"

Mist smiled. A few years in the US was not enough time for the London-born professor to call the tray of cookies *cookies*.

"That's *baking*, not cooking," Mist said.

"Ah, I see." The professor looked at the dessert tray more closely. "Perhaps they need testing."

"They just might," Mist said. "Though Clive tested several this morning when they came out of the oven."

"He's quite adept at that," the professor noted. "I believe he calls it quality control."

Clive's voice entered the café and joined the conversation. "It *is* quality control. It's an important job, and somebody has to be in charge of it." He took another cookie and then turned to Mist.

"Is there any chance you have a few more of your miniature

paintings with the sleigh? I've had a few customers asking for that one. It was the first to run out this year."

"I do have some," Mist said. "I held extras aside for a special project, but I can spare a few. I'll drop them off after breakfast tomorrow."

"Excellent!"

Both Clive and the professor headed to the sandwich station, as did others who chose to either settle at a table or take food in compostable to-go containers that were offered as an option to plates.

Mist was especially pleased to see townsfolk stopping in, many taking meals to go. The Moonglow Café's "pay what your heart tells you" box never fell short of what was needed to feed everyone. Mist knew there were residents able to pay more whose contributions covered those who needed to pay less. It was not unusual to find a crisp one-hundred-dollar bill mixed in with a few crumpled five-dollar bills at the end of the night. And it was not always just monetary efforts that helped feed the town, Mist noted as she watched Sally and Glenda fill several extra boxes on their way through. She knew those boxes were bound for the homes of elderly or disabled residents who couldn't get out to come to the café.

"I see everything is under control. What perfect timing!"

Mist turned to see Michael approaching, his hand firmly holding Rain's hand as she toddled next to him. Both wore coats, gloves—Rain's were actually mittens with cat faces on them that she rarely took off—and warm knit caps with faux fur trim.

Mist bent over and hugged Rain. "Hello, sweet girl. You look cozy and warm!" She stood back up. "You two look like you're going out on a father-daughter polar expedition."

"Maybe we are," Michael said with a glimmer of mischief

in his eyes as he looked around. "And it's a good thing every-thing is under control here."

"And just why is that?"

"Because you're being kidnapped."

Rain looked concerned as she looked up at Michael. "Nap?"

Michael grinned and bent down to kiss the top of her head. "No nap, Rain, not now. Just some fun."

Mist looked at Michael with surprise. "I'm being kid..." She dropped her voice to a whisper. "...*napped?*"

"Yes, you are." Betty, who had just appeared beside them, held Mist's winter cape, a pair of warm gloves, a scarf, and a knit cap. "I'll restock the buffet when needed. Just go enjoy yourself with your family." She politely nudged Mist toward the door of the café, which Mist allowed without much prod-ding. After all, who could resist a surprise kidnapping, espe-cially when it included her two favorite people in the world?

Chapter Twelve

A LIGHT FLURRY OF SNOWFLAKES BRUSHED ACROSS MIST, Michael, and Rain's faces as they walked down the hotel's front walkway. Rain rested in Michael's arms, her head on his shoulder, but she looked up with wide eyes as they reached the waiting sleigh.

For all Mist had pictured the event while in the planning stages, nothing had prepared her for the actual scene she regarded now. The sleigh itself looked like something out of a fairy tale with draped evergreen garlands and gigantic red satin bows. Now, as twilight settled over the town, the tall streetlights at the hotel's fence line cast a magical glow on the decorated sleigh. Christine, dressed as a carriage driver of days gone by, looked as if she'd traveled to Timberton through a time machine. She stood by the horses, who boasted brass bells that reflected the lamplight. Reaching for one of the bell straps, she jiggled it, and the cheerful sound of sleigh bells rang out.

"Pretty horses!" Rain exclaimed.

"Yes, they are!" Mist said. "They're very pretty horses!"

Christine stepped back to allow the three of them to move

closer. "Would you like to say hi to the horses?" She directed the question to Rain but kept an eye on Mist for approval. Both mother and daughter nodded.

"This is Chester, and this is Missy." Christine introduced each horse individually and then winked. "But at Christmastime we call them Chestnut and Mistletoe."

Rain reached out toward the closest horse, and Mist looked questioningly at Christine.

"It's okay," Christine said. "I'll put my hand down first, and she can follow." She placed her hand gently on Chester's neck while speaking to him calmly and then let Rain do the same. When Rain touched the horse, she pulled her hand back and giggled, amused by the texture of the horse's coat.

Once settled in the sleigh, Christine handed each of them one of the bags Mist had decorated and indicated warm blankets by the seats to spread across their laps, which they did while she climbed into the driver's seat. After a cheerful shout of "Are you ready?" the sleigh moved away from the hotel.

With night continuing to fall, they moved into what felt like a magical realm. It was still light enough to see the outline of the trees as they approached the woods just a short distance from the hotel. But it was also dark enough to create an aura of mystery ahead. Soft lights lined the edge of the route the sleigh would follow, and occasional snowflake lights hung from evergreen branches above. Not far ahead, even more lights glowed from the first of many stations along the way. They pulled up to find Marge waiting with a basket of cellophane-wrapped fudge.

"Maple walnut or double chocolate?" Marge inquired with a smile. As they made their choices—maple nut for Mist and double chocolate for Michael—Marge reached deep in the basket and pulled out a third option, which she handed to Rain. "Banana, no sugar," she whispered to Mist, who nodded with appreciation. Marge knew Mist was careful to give Rain natural treats. All three dropped the treats into their bags and thanked Marge.

The horses whinnied and moved forward, once again journeying under shimmering snowflake lights with a view of another station ahead. They arrived to find Ernie from Pop's Parlor, the local watering hole, offering a choice of hot cocoa or a seasonal hot toddy—after all, no one was driving—in lidded cups that would prevent spills while traveling along.

Millie from the library was in charge of the next booth, which was decorated not only with twinkling lights but also images of book covers, all with holiday themes. *A Christmas Carol, How the Grinch Stole Christmas,* and *Polar Express* were all represented along with others. Millie looked the perfect part of an old-time caroler with her wide velvet skirt, waist-length jacket, and vintage-style bonnet tied below her chin. The only hint of modern times was a thick turtleneck under the jacket to provide warmth. She held a stack of pamphlets and slipped one in each bag. "A little Christmas reading for you," she announced with a smile. She waved as they moved on.

Stopping at each station was a delightful experience, and receiving small tokens was naturally part of the fun. But the real joy lay in traveling through a winter wonderland by horse-drawn sleigh and being greeted cheerfully by the townsfolk along the way. Sally had succeeded in pulling her Mrs. Santa Claus costume together, which drew a surprising episode of giggles from Rain as Sally dropped Christmas stickers into each bag. Duffy gave out coupons good for free miniature ice-cream sodas, and Glenda from the Curl 'n' Cue offered candy canes. Yet another station featured carolers—teachers from the local school—who handed out the cellophane bags of Betty's glazed cinnamon nuts. By the time they returned to the hotel after several additional stops, their bags were full of goodies and their hearts were full of joy.

"How was it?" asked the mother of a family next in line. Her two young children wiggled around while eyeing the horses with enthusiasm, and the father held his cell phone, ready to take photos.

"Magical," Mist said. "A memory to treasure." She leaned down to address the children. "Have fun!"

The hotel's front porch was filled with others, some waiting for a sleigh ride and others enjoying hot chocolate and companionship. Holiday music played through outdoor speakers, appropriately starting into "Winter Wonderland." Perfectly timed, Christine shook the strap with bells just as the song reached the opening line of "Sleigh bells ring... are you listening?"

"I think someone is tired." Michael indicated the sleepy girl in his arms, her head resting on his shoulder. "Why don't I take her home? And you can stay to help with the guests."

Mist ran her hand gently over Rain's head, smiling as she watched the young eyes closing halfway between attempts to stay awake. "I think that's an excellent idea. I'll be quite late."

Michael laughed. "I already know that. You have dinner to oversee, then evening activity in the front parlor, then time in your studio room, I'm sure, preparing your surprises for Christmas morning."

"You do know the holiday routine well." Mist gave a kiss to each of her favorite two people, and Michael headed for the short walk to their home, conveniently located in the former Moonglow Café building that Clive had generously and secretly remodeled into a home for them.

Mist stood on the porch for a few minutes after they left. Music and conversation blended together in a perfect duet. And as she stepped back inside, she knew, at least for the moment, that all was well.

Chapter Thirteen

With the extravagant Christmas Eve dinner to follow later that day, breakfast in the café was traditionally a light affair. Guests arrived to find warm slices of apple bread, a bowl of mixed berries, and an assortment of miniature quiches waiting on the buffet. As usual, a side table offered a variety of juices, this time with grapefruit and pineapple as alternatives to orange juice.

As opposed to most mornings at the hotel, this morning meal was reserved for hotel guests only. Many of the townsfolk would join in for the feast later on, so it was reasonable for them to have breakfast at home. This also cut down on kitchen cleanup when there was much to prepare for the dinner event.

Christine was the first to arrive, which surprised Mist considering how exhausted she had to be after leading so many sleigh rides. But she seemed chipper and awake as she helped herself to the buffet.

"I can see you're ready for the day even after all the activity last night," Mist said. She was always pleased to see guests looking forward to a day in Timberton.

"Absolutely," Christine said. "Events like these get my adrenaline flowing. It's so lovely to see people enjoying themselves. I'll crash afterward. Believe me, this is borrowed energy." She chose a table and sat down just as Ivy and the girls entered.

"There she is!" Sage exclaimed as she caught sight of Christine. She skipped over to her table. "You drive the sleigh! Are those your own horses?"

"Yes, they are," Christine said. "They're my best friends too."

Sage thought about this for a few seconds. "Can horses be best friends? I thought a best friend was a person."

"A person could be a best friend." Christine took a sip of grapefruit juice and set her glass down. "But an animal could too."

"Many people consider their pets to be best friends," Ivy said as she and Sienna took places at the table.

"Can we get a best friend horse?" Sage looked at her mother eagerly.

Sienna laughed. "Where would you keep it?"

Sage shrugged. "I don't know."

"We live in an apartment, Sage," Ivy pointed out. "I think it would be a little crowded with a horse in there."

Sienna grinned. "I'm going for food." Sage sighed and followed her sister to the buffet.

Clara and Andrew entered the café next and settled at a large table not far from the front window where they could enjoy the light snowfall that had started sometime during the night. The table was large enough for others to join, which is what the professor did when he arrived. All three made a trip to the buffet and returned to the table. A discussion about British history began, something that had fascinated Andrew since their visit to England. Before long, Diana and Graham joined the others.

Mist circled the room with a pot of coffee in one hand and a cup of the professor's favorite tea in the other.

"You look quite lovely today, my dear Mist," the professor said as she set his tea down and filled Clara's coffee cup.

"Thank you, Professor." Mist smiled. In fact, she did feel rather lovely between the lingering scent of lemon sage shampoo she'd used that morning and the soft burgundy dress that flowed around her work boots. She'd added a vintage reindeer brooch to the dress's cowl neckline for a touch of whimsy, and a retro ivory headband held her hair back from her face.

"Coffee or tea, anyone?" Mist directed the question to all but regarded Diana and Graham first to make sure, as relative newcomers, that they felt a part of the group.

"Coffee would be wonderful!" Diana exclaimed. She held out a mug, and Graham did the same. Mist filled Diana's mug, leaving a little room at the top. She indicated an elegant sugar and creamer set in the shape of white Christmas trees with gold detail.

Diana took a cautious sip of coffee while Mist filled Graham's mug. "I saw your paintings at the gallery yesterday, Mist. They're wonderful, and I love that you make miniatures. They could fit in anyone's home as opposed to large pieces that require wall space."

"Thank you," Mist said. "Painting brings me joy, and I want anyone to be able to enjoy them regardless of the size of their home."

"I used to paint," Diana said so quietly that Mist barely heard her over the happy chatter of other guests around the room.

"Used to," Mist repeated gently. "You don't anymore?"

Diana shook her head. "I'm not sure why I stopped. I just

hit a slump and stopped. I suppose I became dissatisfied with what I was painting and didn't want to keep disappointing myself."

"She was very good," Graham said as he stood and eyed the buffet.

"You lost the joy," Mist suggested.

"I suppose so," Diana said. "I never thought of it exactly that way."

"Perhaps you'll start again."

"Perhaps." Diana set her coffee down, her expression contemplative, and stood to join Graham. They both headed to the buffet. Mist moved on to other tables and then returned to the kitchen.

"You look deep in thought," Betty said as she looked over an assortment of vegetables and fruit that lay next to a cutting board on the center island. Mist was grateful for the hotelkeeper's offer to help prep food for the dinner later. Much was already prepared, but there were always same-day tasks.

"You're right. I am," Mist replied. She set the coffeepot she'd been carrying down on a burner and took a seat across from Betty.

Betty picked up a pear and waved it in the air. "I don't have a penny, but how about a pear for your thoughts?"

Mist laughed. "We need those pears for the pear pomegranate salad tonight. But I'm happy to share my thoughts anyway. I was thinking about joy—how we lose it and how we regain it."

"And what brought this on?" Betty asked as she cut a pear in half and then quarters.

"A conversation with one of the guests about how she used to love painting and then stopped. I could tell she misses it."

"Then I hope she starts again someday," Betty said. She set one pear aside, picked up another, and began to slice it.

Mist nodded. "I do too. But it does make me wonder... what makes us regain that joy after we lose it?"

Betty shrugged. "Some kind of inspiration, I guess."

"You're absolutely right, Betty. Thank you."

Mist moved to the refrigerator and took out a selection of romaine, green leaf, and butter lettuce. She set it by the sink and turned on the water, letting it run over her fingers before commencing to wash the mixed greens. *Yes*, she thought as she worked her way through the crisp produce. Getting joy back again after losing it was a question of inspiration. And what better time for inspiration than Christmas?

Chapter Fourteen

The side door to the kitchen opened, and Maisie stepped in, bringing a quick flurry of snowflakes with her. She shut the door quickly and exhaled, obviously pleased to step into the warmth of the hotel.

"Any way I can help? I thought I could escape the holiday craziness at my house for an hour or so." Maisie removed her hat and gloves without waiting for an answer. "Clayton's mother has set up a drum set of pots and pans for Cora, Clay and his father have sports on the television, and Clay Jr. is running around pretending to be a pirate. Every ten seconds he jumps in front of everyone and shouts 'Ahoy, me hearties!'"

Betty and Mist both laughed, picturing the scene.

"I love it all, of course," Maisie continued. "But sometimes a short sanity break is in order." She slipped out of her coat and hung it on a wall hook.

"Understandable!" Betty exclaimed.

Mist set aside a tray of fingerling potatoes she had just washed. "Actually, that would be wonderful. I promised Clive I'd run a few more paintings down to the gallery."

"Excellent!" Maisie said. "You can be the art monitor, and I'll be on potato patrol. What do these need?"

"Just a bit of olive oil and some seasonings." Mist pointed to the various ingredients on the counter. "But you don't have to do anything. I won't be at the gallery long."

"Nonsense," Maisie replied. "This is a treat for me. You know I love helping here in this kitchen."

Betty nodded. "It's true, Mist. Knowing we're feeding others makes this all the more enjoyable. Which reminds me to get out the containers we use to deliver food to those who can't make it here to the café."

"I can set those up," Maisie said. "I know where you keep them."

"Thanks," Mist said. "We're adding a square of fudge from Marge's shop to those tonight. She's making it this morning. I'll pick it up on the way back from the gallery so she doesn't need to drop it off."

Mist thanked Maisie and Betty for their help, picked up the box of miniature paintings from the back studio room, and headed out.

The walk to Clive's gallery was approximately two blocks, and it passed almost all the businesses in the small town. Between the falling snow and the holiday lights and decorations in windows, it seemed like walking through a magical winter wonderland. Townsfolk out for either last-minute shopping or to drop small gifts off made the town feel alive. Mist was delighted to have an excuse to experience it. She smiled as she observed the line inside Marge's candy shop and felt an unexpected rush of childhood joy at the sight of the train in Duffy's window.

Not all businesses were open. Sally's thrift shop was closed for a holiday vacation. Glenda at the Curl 'n' Cue had told people they could get their hair and nails done by the twenty-third or wait until the twenty-seventh, though she had to convince a few customers that they would survive seventy-two hours without those services.

A cupboard outside Maisie's Daisies held an assortment of flower arrangements with an honor-system box for payment. She would later be asked if she'd lost money by setting that up, and she would reply that there was more in the box than the arrangements would have normally cost. This was surprising to some people but not to Mist. People were generous in a town where taking care of each other was the norm.

Clive's gallery was moderately busy with a few customers browsing the art section while others looked at jewelry items. Mist recognized a few of the patrons, including Ivy, who held a bag she'd just been handed by Addison. She greeted Mist with enthusiasm.

"I'm having such a wonderful time here," Ivy said. "The girls are so happy. They weren't very enthusiastic about taking a trip for the holidays. It meant missing activities with their friends. But between the sleigh rides and the wonderful crafts table you have in the front parlor, they're having a blast."

Mist smiled, knowing this was the goal all along. The experience of Christmas in Timberton needed to offer a heartwarming experience for all ages. And now that she was a mother herself, she realized how much that meant to parents. Happy children meant happy parents.

Ivy headed out with her small bag from the jewelry section. Mist had made a point of not asking what she'd purchased. She had an idea that she suspected was correct. If so, she'd find out on Christmas morning.

Addison, who'd taken a break between customers at the front register, met Mist at the back table that served as an office of sorts. Mist placed the box of miniature paintings on the desk.

"Wonderful," Addison exclaimed. "We have a few empty

wall hooks in that area, which always looks odd. Now to just get a chance to hang these." She glanced at the front register, and Mist did the same. Another customer had approached and now waited.

"I can do that," Mist offered immediately. "I've included a list of what I brought, so Clive will know what to adjust in inventory."

"Thank you!" Addison rushed back up front.

Mist walked around to the wall where her paintings were displayed in a patchwork arrangement that always reminded Mist of a quilt. Seeing several empty hooks, she hung the sleigh paintings and then rearranged a few to allow the patterns to be separated. A sleigh hung next to a winter forest scene, the winter forest scene shared a space beside a gingerbread house, and the gingerbread house flanked a bright red cardinal on a snowy evergreen branch. She stood back, pleased with the arrangement.

"So these are your paintings," a voice nearby said. "I love them."

Mist turned to see Diana a few feet away. Graham was not far from her, admiring a larger painting of the town by a local artist. His camera hung from his shoulder, and he was respectful enough of the artists to not be photographing their artwork.

"Thank you, Diana."

"This trip is making me want to paint again. I'm not quite sure what it is." Diana stepped closer and looked over the varied scenes.

"I think there could be a lot of reasons," Mist suggested. "I've always suspected that travel leads to inspiration, almost as if we can see things inside us that we can't see at home."

"I think you're right," Diana replied. "Life at home is filled with everyday tasks. It's easy to stay busy with things that have to get done: errands, house chores, interactions with friends and neighbors. Not to mention jobs. There's always something. I've become very wrapped up in all of that over the years. External things as opposed to internal."

Mist understood all too well. She adored her life in Timberton, but it could be busy. On the few trips that she and Michael had taken, she'd been able to look inward more as well as observe what existed outside of her daily experiences.

Leaving Diana to enjoy the gallery, she slipped out the front door. She paused just outside to close her eyes and feel the cool brush of snow across her face, wanting to take in the sensation by itself. Content with the brief pause, she continued on to Marge's, where she picked up the individually packaged maple walnut fudge that would go in the dinner deliveries later on. Clara was in line to pick up something sweet for Andrew—he was fond of Marge's cashew turtle clusters—as well as a small gift of caramels for Betty.

Mist returned to the hotel to find not only was all well in the kitchen but the fingerling potatoes were ready to go in the oven later, the salad was finished, covered, and stored in the downstairs refrigerator, and all the ingredients for the boeuf bourguignon were laid out on the counter, waiting for Mist's special chef's touch. It would cook for several hours, during which time she'd put together side dishes. In addition, the place settings were perfectly arranged in the café.

"Maisie went back home," Betty said as she set a bottle of Pinot Noir next to the other ingredients. "And I'm off to do a few last-minute Christmas tasks if you don't need me for anything."

"Please go," Mist said, immediately laughing when she realized what her quick statement sounded like. "I don't mean it like that! I mean you've already helped so much. I'm just going to get this glorious French stew cooking and get the side dishes together."

As Betty headed out, Mist looked around the kitchen, taking in the relative quiet. A distant background of holiday music and happy chatter flowed from the front parlor. With everyone out and about, she was free to do one of her favorite things of all, to prepare food for others to enjoy. And so with a sense of peace, she let herself enjoy every minute.

Chapter Fifteen

If Mist were to be asked what moment of the year was always the most magical to her, she'd likely say it was just before opening the café doors for the Christmas Eve dinner. Whether it was the anticipation or the tradition or simply the surroundings, this was always when she sensed a unique stirring of spirit. It was one moment she kept just for herself—though she now shared it with Rain—lingering inside the closed doors of the café, a communion with the event about to take place.

Looking around the candlelit café now, she was pleased with the ambiance the guests would soon enjoy. Tapered candles on each table rose above the floral sleigh arrangements, casting flickering light across the tabletops. Tiny white lights twinkled from green garlands along the front of the buffet as others dangled from the ceiling. Smooth jazz renditions of classic Christmas carols flowed from the speaker system. And the aromas of roasted garlic, caramelized onions, rosemary and thyme, and a hint of ginger wafted through the room.

"You see, Rain?" she whispered to the sweet child on her hip. "This is what people will enjoy tonight. Isn't it pretty?"

"So pretty!" Rain said, waving an arm out toward the room.

"Just like you, my wonderful girl." Mist ran her free hand softly over Rain's hair, enthralled as she always was with its silken texture. "What do you say we let others come in and enjoy it?" She nodded, and Rain nodded in return.

Mist moved to the café entrance, setting Rain down before opening the doors. She brushed the front of her own red silk and ivory lace dress, and Rain copied her movement on her own similar yet more washable version of her mother's dress. Both wore ivory headbands with rhinestones that picked up the candlelight as well as the tiny white lights that sparkled from the ceiling. It was an enchanting scene, and they were ready to share it. Mist and Rain—Mist a little more than Rain, of course—then opened the café doors to enthusiastic cheers from those waiting.

One of the many wonderful things about Christmas Eve dinner at the Moonglow Café was the mix of local residents and hotel guests. It was always crowded in a wonderfully joyous way. Townsfolk knew this was the case, and many chose to arrive at different times to make seating people less challenging. But no matter who happened to attend at the same time, the sharing of stories between guests and townsfolk added a new dimension to the guest experience. They weren't just seeing the town; they were able to become a part of it for that evening. In the same manner, residents of Timberton had a chance to hear tales of places far away, whether other states or even other countries. This, to Mist, was the wonder of it all. Not the elegant dinner itself, not the festive decorations and ambiance, delightful as everything was. It was the gathering of people together to share stories, experiences, and laughter.

Ivy and the girls were the first to arrive, all wearing

sweaters with holiday designs. The professor soon followed, sporting evening attire and the usual bow tie he liked to don for special occasions. Michael accompanied him but waved him on toward the tables. He lingered with Mist at the door, taking Rain into his arms.

Wild Bill and Sally stepped in next along with Clayton and the two children, Clay Jr. and little Cora, who smiled at the sight of Rain. The two girls had continued to form a friendship, being only a month apart in age. Clayton would save a place for Maisie, who was helping in the kitchen.

Others from the town arrived, as did Diana and Graham. Mist remained by the café doors to greet people. Christine was the very last to arrive, having needed time to get the horses settled back in the barn after the final sleigh ride. To her surprise, a round of applause broke out as she stepped into the café.

"You made a lot of people happy on those sleigh rides," Mist said.

"They made *me* happy," Christine replied. "What could be more heartwarming than watching people set their cares aside and enjoy the moment?"

Mist looked around the room and had to agree. The world was full of challenges, but there were still moments that allowed worries to be set aside. The Christmas Eve dinner was certainly one of them.

As the room filled, so did the sounds that accompanied a crowded café: cheerful conversation, chairs sliding out and back in as people headed to and from the buffet, glasses clinking as toasts to the holiday crossed tables. Michael and Rain took seats at a table with Clayton's family, which allowed Rain and Cora to converse insofar as seventeen- and eighteen-month-old young ladies can. Clay Jr. sat beside Cora, having taken on a caring big-brother role over the past year and a half.

"Have you gotten some good pictures?" Clara asked Graham as he sat down with a hearty assortment of fare from the buffet. He'd rarely been seen without his camera, whether hanging from his shoulder or focused intently on a subject.

"I think so." Graham appeared pleased. "I've been reviewing them at night. I believe I've captured your charming town fairly well. Which hasn't been difficult. There's something picturesque in every direction. It would be a challenge *not* to get good pictures."

"It really is charming here," Diana said. "We've never had a Christmas quite like this. We've always either been at home in Manhattan or away in another city somewhere. Never anywhere like Timberton."

"I'm not sure there's anywhere quite like Timberton," Clara said. "And we travel a lot. But I think small towns in general have a different feeling than cities do. They feel friendlier."

"Indeed." The professor spoke up from the next table. "The lack of anonymity counts for part of it, I believe."

"Yes," Clara agreed. "In a city, you can walk around all day and not run into someone you know. That would never happen here."

Clive laughed. "That's for sure. You might walk around here all day and not run into anyone you *didn't* know."

"That's even true for visitors," Ivy said. "We've had several people around town ask how we're enjoying our visit."

"I love everyone here," Sage announced. "Especially Bacon." She looked around and caught the pup's attention where he rested below a nearby table where Hollister dined. Sticking a fork in a tender piece of beef, she quietly lowered her arm beside her chair. As if in on a secret between just the two of them, Bacon emerged just long enough to gobble the treat down before retreating innocently back under the table.

"Oh, I dropped my fork!" Sage said. Having let it slip out of her hand once Bacon had finished his tender treat.

Sienna rolled her eyes. "I'll get you another one." Ivy exchanged looks with Sage, whether because she knew what her daughter had pulled off or not.

By the time dessert rolled around, appetites had been satisfied but many a sweet tooth remained. Mist and Maisie together worked to serve small portions of gingerbread bundt cake—some as small as one bite, others larger—with fresh whipped cream added for those who wanted it. At Michael and Clayton's insistence, Mist and Maisie both sat down with their own small portions once everyone had been served.

"An outstanding dinner, as always," Clayton said, setting his fork down in surrender. Clay Jr., who regularly followed in his father's steps, did the same.

"Thank you, Clay," Mist said. "It was a group effort, I assure you." She turned to Maisie. "I couldn't do it without you." Maisie, Cora now on her lap and her own mouth full of gingerbread, nodded in appreciation. Mist knew she loved helping out.

One by one, table by table, the crowd in the café lightened as many locals returned home, and others, as well as hotel guests, moved into the front parlor to continue their time together.

Mist helped clean up as much as possible before she was shooed out of the kitchen by others offering to help. She made sure the lobby's beverage center—coffee, tea, hot chocolate, and hot mulled cider—was fully stocked along with Betty's glazed cinnamon nuts and an assortment of cookies from the cookie exchange. After which, encouraged by Michael, she moved into the front parlor to enjoy the post-dinner activity.

Chapter Sixteen

There was always a unique feeling to the after-dinner gathering in the front parlor on Christmas Eve. Maybe it was the anticipation of Christmas itself or perhaps it was a result of guests getting to know each other over the past few days. Or it could even be the subconscious knowing that they'd be departing soon and returning to their own homes and lives. It just always felt a little different from other nights.

Clive had kept the fire going, even taking a trip in the middle of dinner to add a couple of logs. Now, as guests and townsfolk alike moved into the room, he was about to add another log when Mist approached.

"Why don't you let Michael handle the fire while you take his place?" She waited while Clive looked around, spotting Michael in his usual place by the fire, Rain in his lap. As she expected, his face lit up. He'd been a grandfather figure ever since Rain was born.

"I'm not sure my beard can take it," he said, grinning. "But I'd love to." Without hesitation, he and Michael traded places. To no one's surprise, Rain crawled right up on Clive's lap and pulled his beard. It was a game they'd played since she first started reaching for things. She'd pull, he'd react with mock surprise, she'd pull again, and so it continued until they both fell into wild laughter.

True to tradition, there was always someone in the crowd who possessed some keyboard magic, and this year, to the surprise of many, it turned out to be Duffy who slid onto the piano bench and let his fingers fly.

"Oh my!" Clara exclaimed from her seat on the couch. "He's good! He's really good!"

Sally, standing close enough to hear Clara, leaned over and whispered, "It's rather a not-well-kept secret that he has a piano in the back room of his store. You can hear him play late at night."

Mist, overhearing this, smiled. It was true. Many a night she'd walked down there to listen outside, behind the store. And she wasn't the only one. Several outdoor chairs had appeared over time, set back as to not be noticeable.

Duffy launched into a medley of upbeat Christmas carols, creating a challenge for those who had gathered around the piano to sing. He jumped from one song to another unexpectedly to see how quickly the singers could switch. Hearty laughter accompanied the attempts to hop from half a verse of "Frosty the Snowman" to the chorus of "Feliz Navidad" to a full verse of "Joy to the World." Duffy threw in bits of musical embellishment along the way. Mist was especially pleased to see Hollister join in by resting his hand on top of the piano in order to feel the beat of the music. Bacon, by his side, added his own voice to the mix with a cheerful howl now and then.

"Everyone looks relaxed and cheerful," Betty said as she came to stand by Mist. "And I see the craft table is quite busy too. The girls are there, Ivy is there, and even Diana is there."

Mist smiled. "Yes, she is." As she'd hoped, the sketch pad

and watercolors she'd quietly added to the table had caught Diana's eye. She'd passed by casually and noticed the supplies had not been overlooked. While Graham was wandering around the room with his camera, Diana had started creating a Christmas scene, choosing—likely per a suggestion from both girls—a sleigh ride as the subject.

"I see Clara and Andrew over by the Christmas tree now," Betty whispered with a secretive smile, which Mist returned. They had slowly figured out over the years that the travel aficionados had been sneaking a small ornament onto the tree each year. They waited until the two had wandered away and then sauntered over to see what they might have added.

"There's the little pyramid ornament they added last year," Mist pointed out. "The one that made us realize they'd been sneaking them in."

Betty reached into the tree to point out another. "And the pineapple from Maui." She touched another one, a miniature pair of wooden shoes. "This one they gave to us directly the year they went to the Netherlands."

"I've always loved that one," Mist said. "Of course, I love the whole concept of our tree with the varied ornaments: some from your family collection, some gifts, and some handmade by schoolchildren here in town."

"I agree. It lets the tree tell a story."

"Many stories," Mist clarified.

A deeper voice entered the conversation as Clive joined them. "And I know one of those stories. I think it's known as when the guy gets the girl."

Mist was charmed to see Betty blush as Clive reached into the far depths of the tree where he hid a custom-designed orna-ment each year. She never knew if Betty managed to sneak a look at it early, but he never added it to the tree until the

Christmas Eve dinner, so there was a good chance it was a surprise.

"And for this year," he announced with enough dramatic flair to make Mist imagine a drumroll, "we add this to the collection." Betty's face lit up when she saw the dangling silver sleigh. A swirling ribbon boasted tiny Yogo sapphires representing sleigh bells, accents he added to all the ornaments he made for her.

"I love it," Betty exclaimed. She gave Clive a sweet kiss and then reached into the tree with the sparkling ornament. "I'm going to put it here between last year's angel and the snowflake from a few years ago." She chose a spot on a branch and let it hang free. "Thank you, Clive."

"Anything for my girl." Clive put his arm around her and pulled her close before moving out to visit with others around the room.

Ivy and both girls approached the tree next, and Ivy picked out two boxes and handed them to the girls. "We don't open presents on Christmas Eve in general," she offered by way of explanation. "But this is the one exception, a tradition we have."

Mist and Betty watched as Sage and Sienna opened the packages and pulled out sets of pajamas. "These are awesome!" Sage exclaimed as she admired the Grinch-themed pattern. "I love the Grinch."

Duffy, overhearing the comment, immediately launched into a rendition of "You're a Mean One, Mr. Grinch," which sent both girls into a fit of giggles.

"This way they can wake up in them on Christmas morning," Ivy explained to Betty and Mist.

"Excellent idea," Betty said to Ivy before turning to the girls. "You're both going to look so stylish and festive."

"Speaking of Christmas morning..." Mist let the statement

trail off as she looked around. Guests crowded around the fireplace with drinks of one sort or another. Sage and Sienna had returned to the crafts table, where Diana remained focused on painting. Duffy continued to entertain the crowd. Joy was present throughout the room.

"Go," Betty whispered, knowing Mist always had her own special project to finish on Christmas Eve. "I'll keep the beverages stocked, including the hot mulled cider."

Knowing everything was under control, Mist slipped out of the room. She listened as the cheerful mix of music and conversation faded behind her. By the time she reached her studio room and closed the door, there was only silence, which was exactly what she needed. Just as she did every year, she had a project to finish, one that would send guests off with a reminder of their Christmas in Timberton.

Chapter Seventeen

Christmas morning dawned glorious, a crystal-clear sky above sending rays of sunshine down onto the freshly fallen snow of the night before.

Mist had already set the coffee to brew and cranberry scones to bake long before the sun rose over Timberton. Guests were bound to rise earlier than usual. This particular morning always carried a sense of expectation, even for adults. Perhaps it was the remnants of childhood that inevitably lingered regardless of a person's age. On the other hand, those still in the realm of youth were guaranteed to appear at an early hour. So it was no surprise when Mist heard the sound of light footsteps and whispers coming down the stairs.

Peeking out into the lobby from the café door where she'd been straightening the buffet, she was not surprised to see Sage and Sienna tiptoeing up to the Christmas tree. Indeed, there were gifts under the tree that hadn't been there the night before when they'd opened their pajamas. Ivy had added other packages that she'd shipped ahead of time. Betty had hidden them in a back room until the night before, when she moved them to the café so Ivy could transfer them to the tree sometime during the night. Other guests had added to the assortment of gifts, including those that Mist had slipped in between the branches the night before.

Clive was one of the first to appear, heading first for coffee and then to the kitchen. It had become somewhat of a tradition for him to help prepare breakfast on Christmas Day. On this particular morning, those contributions would come in the form of turtles, giraffes, and bears—all formed with pancake batter, of course. These were always a crowd pleaser with children, and more than one adult had been known to order up a critter of some sort. Whatever might be requested from Clive's "zoo" this morning, it would be accompanied by other choices from the buffet: a breakfast frittata, honeydew melon slices, and homemade granola. Some would choose a light selection, still full from the feast the night before. Others would have regained their appetite after a good night's sleep.

Ivy and the girls were soon to follow, though it might have been more appropriate to phrase it as "the girls and Ivy." The daughters were noticeably more awake than their mother, something that surely matched many households on this particular holiday. Ivy helped herself to coffee while the girls picked a table. By the time she sat down with them, they had already placed their breakfast order.

"Coming right up," Clive said as he pretended to write their order on an invisible notepad. "One elephant and one rhinoceros. Anything for you, Ivy?"

"Just keep the coffee flowing." Ivy yawned.

"We can manage that." Clive added it to the invisible order pad and headed for the kitchen.

"One of you ordered a rhinoceros?" Ivy asked, looking between the girls.

Sage nodded. "I did."

"Clive said they were all out of alligators," Sienna explained.

"Well then, that makes sense." Ivy brought her coffee cup to her lips.

Christmas morning breakfast at the Moonglow Café was limited to hotel guests, so it wasn't long before the group had all gathered. Diana and Graham joined Clara and Andrew, and the professor took a seat with Ivy and the girls, charming all of them—though possibly not Clive—by ordering an octopus. "Wearing a hat," he had added just to give Clive a hard time.

Christine helped herself to some granola and melon slices at the buffet and sat with Michael and Rain, soon to be joined by Mist, who had been nudged out of the kitchen by both Betty and Clive so she could enjoy the morning meal with the guests and family.

Over coffee, tea, frittata, melon, granola, and a zoo full of pancakes, guests visited with each other, finding, as often happened at the Timberton Hotel, that they'd come to know each other over the few days they'd spent together. Evidence of that showed as they moved from breakfast into the front parlor and relaxed, surrounded with holiday music, a warm fire, and a picture-perfect Christmas tree.

Sage and Sienna opened a variety of gifts first, and then Ivy handed them small velvet bags with drawstring ribbons. The elegant bags fit in the palms of their hands.

"What are these?" Sage said, holding her hand open as if she'd discovered magic treasure.

"Just something extra," Ivy said. She exchanged a glance with Clive as she watched the girls open the bags.

"It's a charm for our bracelets!" Sienna announced. She smiled and held up the tiny silver sleigh as Sage did the same.

"From Clive's magic workshop," Ivy said.

Clive smiled, pleased that he'd added a sleigh to his custom designs back when the sleigh ride activity was first suggested.

Others exchanged gifts, though some had opted not to. Clara and Andrew always considered their travels to be gifts to each other. Diana and Graham held the same philosophy, though Graham had been yearning for a particular camera not yet released. Michael gave the professor a vintage copy of Steinbeck's *The Grapes of Wrath,* and the professor in return gave Michael a similar copy of Agatha Christie's *Murder in Three Acts* since Michael had recently developed a penchant for mysteries.

Graham surprised everyone by passing out photos of each group on the sleigh rides, printed with a portable printer that he carried with him.

Mist and Michael had not surprisingly chosen to direct all gift-giving to Rain. Though they kept most of her presents at home, Rain did have one to open at the hotel, which she tore into with remarkable glee and then held up a bright tie-dyed dress for all to see.

As was a Christmas tradition at the hotel, Mist pulled several small packages from between the branches of the tree, handing them out to the new guests. Diana and Graham opened theirs together and both smiled when they held up the miniature painting of a sleigh. An easel and paintbrushes filled one end, and the other boasted a camera and tripod.

"It appears you have a creative year ahead of you," Ivy said. "That's wonderful."

"Yes," Diana said as she and Graham admired the painting. "It really is."

Mist handed Ivy her package, and she opened it, delighted to find a painting of a sleigh with two girls in it. "This is a perfect memory of this trip," she exclaimed. "Thank you, Mist. The girls absolutely loved the sleigh ride."

With no warning, both girls burst into laughter after removing the wrapping from their gifts, which baffled everyone but Mist. It was only somewhat explained when they turned their paintings out for everyone to see.

"Very clever, Mist," Christine said, understanding immediately,

"They're getting to ride!" Sage exclaimed. "The horses get to go for a sleigh ride!" She and Sienna collapsed into laughter again.

Mist handed out the last gift, which went to Christine. She opened it quickly and grinned. "Chester and Missy thank you," she said, holding up the painting of a sleigh overflowing with carrots.

"That's a lot of carrots," Sage said, barely recovering from her laughing fit.

Christine nodded. "Yes, it is, and I'm sure they'll eat every one of them."

"But not on the same day," Sienna pointed out.

"No," Christine said. "Not on the same day."

"Quite lucky these horses are," the professor noted. "A sleigh ride and a rather large aggregation of carrots."

"And speaking of sleigh rides..." Christine said as she stood up. "I believe I hear two horses calling my name. Will I see anyone here out on the trail today? We have marvelous weather." She glanced out the front window, and others did the same.

A chorus of enthusiastic replies gave her the answer. And so guests scattered in various directions, some gathering warm coats and others settling down for indoor activities. But one thing was constant among them all: a joyous Christmas Day.

Chapter Eighteen

Mist stood with Betty on the front porch, and they both waved as the last of the departing guests pulled away from the curb. The day after Christmas always seemed a bit melancholy. This year's guests had become—as many had over the years—a part of the hotel's holiday family. Although there was joy in seeing them refreshed and returning to their regular lives, Mist always felt a little wistful to see them leave.

"I feel the same," Betty said as if reading Mist's thoughts.

"There will be others next Christmas," Mist pointed out.

"Yes."

"And the Christmas after that," Mist added.

"Yes."

Mist wrapped her arms around herself and stepped forward on the porch, looking off in one direction and then in another. "There's something marvelous in meeting new people. You never know quite what to expect."

Betty laughed. "You mean like this crazy man coming up the front walk right now?"

"I heard that," Clive said as he climbed the porch steps. "If I'm crazy, why did you marry me?"

"Maybe I like crazy," Betty said as she and Clive exchanged a kiss. "How's your after-Christmas sale going at the gallery?"

"Busy but not unmanageable," Clive said. "I'm going right back to help Addison after I grab something for lunch."

Betty slipped her hand inside his arm and guided him to the front door. "I'll put something together quickly that you can take back."

Clive grinned. "That's my girl."

"Coming in, Mist?" Betty asked.

"Not quite yet."

Mist remained on the porch and was soon joined by Michael and Rain, who climbed into Mist's arms and wrapped her arms around her mother's neck.

"Another Timberton Christmas in the books," Michael said. "Are you feeling the post-holiday blues?"

"Not too much," Mist replied, most of her answer going into Rain's hair. "The year will fly by as it always does. And then it will be Christmas again."

Michael reached over and pulled a strand of Rain's hair off Mist's mouth, which caused them both to laugh. This in turn caused Rain to laugh, creating an endearing picture of the young family to a few townsfolk passing by.

"It'll be a busy year," Michael noted. "Can you believe we'll have a two-and-a-half-year-old this time next year?"

Mist placed a kiss on top of Rain's head. "Yes, I believe it. And a three-and-a-half-year-old the year after that. But let's not rush ahead in our minds. Those days will come soon enough."

"Indeed, they will," Michael said.

Mist looked out at the sweet scene of the town before them. Two elderly residents waved as they walked by with bright new hats and scarves received as Christmas presents. A child accompanied a father pulling a sled, both headed for a hill a few blocks away. The snowfall had lightened overnight, but slight wisps of snow still fell, mixed with occasional teases of sunlight.

"Yes," Mist said, aware what Michael meant because she felt exactly the same way. "Those days will come soon enough. And we'll be right here."

Betty's Cookie Exchange Recipes

Glazed Cinnamon Nuts
Carrot Cake Cookies
Cherry Bars
Cinnamon-Oatmeal Breakfast Bites
Strawberry Crumbles
Cannoli Cookies
Pumpkin Chocolate-Chip Cookies
Raspberry Swirl Cookies
Fresh Apple Cake
Cherry Bell Christmas Cookies
Potato Chip Cookies
Chocolate Truffles
Fruitcake Cookies
First Day of School Cookies
Gingerbread Snowball Cookies
Christmas Butter Cookies
Peanut Butter Chocolate Chip Cookies
Peanut Butter Snowballs
Orange Cranberry Ricotta Cookies
Nana's Kitchen Sink Cookies
Snowy Winter Moons

Glazed Cinnamon Nuts
(a family recipe)

Ingredients:
    1 cup sugar
    1/4 cup water
    1/8 teaspoon cream of tartar
    Heaping teaspoon of cinnamon
    1 tablespoon butter
    1-1/2 cups walnut halves

Directions:
Boil sugar, water, cream of tartar, and cinnamon to soft boil stage (236°).

Remove from heat. Add butter and walnuts.

Stir until walnuts separate. Place on waxed paper to cool.

Carrot Cake Cookies
(Submitted by Lena Winfrey Hayat)

Ingredients:

    1 cup light brown sugar

    1 cup granulated sugar

    1 cup (2 sticks) unsalted butter (room temp)

    2 large eggs (room temp)

    1 teaspoon vanilla extract

    2 cups all-purpose flour

    1 teaspoon baking powder

    1 teaspoon baking soda

    1/4 teaspoon salt

    1 teaspoon ground cinnamon

    1/2 teaspoon ground ginger

    1/2 teaspoon ground nutmeg

    2 cups rolled oats

    1 1/2 cups finely grated carrots (3 large carrots)

    1 cup raisins

    1/2 cup walnuts (finely chopped) optional

*Cream Cheese Frosting (filling between the cookies; recipe at the end)

Directions:

Use an electric mixer on medium speed to beat together butter, brown sugar, and granulated sugar until fluffy (about 3 to 4 minutes). Add eggs and vanilla and beat on medium speed until well mixed.

Sift together flour, baking powder, baking soda, salt, cinnamon, ginger and nutmeg. Stir to combine. Add flour mixture gradually to the butter mixture. Mix on low speed until it's blended. Mix in carrots, oats, raisins, and walnuts, which are optional. Chill mixture for one hour until firm.

Preheat the oven to 350 degrees. Shape tablespoons of dough into balls. Place cookie balls two inches apart on two baking sheets covered with parchment paper.

Bake cookies for 7 minutes and then turn them over. Bake for another 6 to 8 minutes, until brown and crispy. Move cookies to a wire rack to cool. Then, using a spatula, spread two teaspoons of the cream cheese frosting onto the flat sides of half the cookies. Then sandwich the other half of the cookies onto them.

Cookies can be refrigerated in an airtight container for up to three days. Recipe yields three dozen cookies.

Cream Cheese Frosting:
    8 oz. cream cheese, room temperature
    1/2 cup (one stick) unsalted butter, room temperature
    1 cup powdered sugar
    1 teaspoon vanilla extract

Directions:
Put cream cheese in a mixing bowl and with a rubber spatula, beat cream cheese until smooth. Add gradually butter and keep beating until it's well blended. Then, sift in powdered sugar and beat until smooth. Finally, add vanilla and mix well.

Cherry Bars
(Submitted by Kay McCarter Pflueger)

Ingredients:
    1 cup butter, softened
    2 cups sugar
    1 teaspoon salt
    4 large eggs
    1 teaspoon vanilla extract
    1/4 teaspoon almond extract
    3 cups all-purpose flour
    2 cans (21 ounces each) cherry pie filling

Glaze:
    1 cup confectioners' sugar
    1/2 teaspoon vanilla extract
    1/2 teaspoon almond extract
    2 to 3 tablespoons whole milk

Directions:
    Preheat oven to 350°
    In a large bowl, cream butter, sugar, and salt until light and fluffy.
    Add eggs, one at a time, beating well after each addition.
    Beat in extracts. Gradually add flour.
    Spread 3 cups dough into a greased 15 x 10 x 1-in. baking pan.
    Spread with pie filling. Drop remaining dough by teaspoonfuls over filling.
    Bake 35-40 minutes or until golden brown.
    Cool completely in pan on a wire rack.
    In a small bowl, mix confectioners' sugar, extracts, and enough milk to reach desired consistency. Drizzle over top.

Cinnamon Oat Breakfast Bites
(Submitted by Annie Sarac)

Ingredients:
    2-1/2 cups oats
    1 tablespoon cinnamon
    1 tablespoon brown sugar
    1/4 teaspoon allspice or pumpkin spice
    2 teaspoon baking powder
    4 tablespoon butter, melted
    4 ounces unsweetened applesauce
    1 banana
    16 ounces of ice cream

Directions:

Measure two cups of oats into a mixing bowl. Open ice cream carton and set aside. Taste the ice cream to make sure the flavor will balance with cinnamon. Set aside brown sugar.

Mix in baking powder, spice, and cinnamon. Cleanse your palate with two tablespoons ice cream.

Stir in applesauce, syrup, and melted butter. Squish in a banana if you are really feeling wild. Measure a fourth cup of ice cream and consume to determine if the temperature is adequate.

Press mixture into an eight-by-ten glass dish. Sprinkle a thin layer of brown sugar on top. Refresh palate with one-third cup ice cream.

Bake for twenty minutes at 350 degrees. While you are waiting, savor one cup ice cream as quality control.

Insert knife into mix to see if it's done. Cut into squares and place on a pretty plate. Add remaining ice cream on top because no one puts leftover ice cream back in the freezer.

Enjoy with a Scottish mystery.

Strawberry Crumbles
(Submitted by Petrenia Etheridge)

Ingredients:
    1 box strawberry cake mix
    1 egg
    1/4 cup avocado oil
    1/4 cup melted butter
    1 cup chopped strawberries, fresh or frozen

Glaze
    1 cup powdered sugar
    1-2 tablespoons milk

Directions:
Mix in first 4 ingredients well then fold in strawberries. Mixture will be thick.

Roll into 1-2 inch balls and place on parchment paper. Press down slightly with the bottom of a greased or wet glass.

Bake at 350 until lightly brown, 9-10 minutes. Let cool.

Mix glaze and spread or drizzle over top of cookies.

Yield: 2 inch balls = 18 cookies

Cannoli Cookies
(Submitted by Patti Rusk)

Cannoli Cookies bring all the flavors of a cannoli to a soft, delicious cookie! With creamy ricotta, mini chocolate chips, and a dusting of powdered sugar, these cookies are perfect for holidays or anytime.

Ingredients:

1/2 cup (1 stick) unsalted butter, softened
1 cup drained ricotta cheese * (see below)
3/4 cup granulated sugar
1 large egg
1 teaspoon vanilla extract
1 3/4 cups all-purpose flour
1/2 teaspoon baking powder
1/4 teaspoon salt
1/2 cup mini chocolate chips
Powdered sugar, for dusting

Directions:

Preheat your oven to 350°F. Line baking sheets with parchment paper or silicone baking mats to prevent sticking.

In a large mixing bowl, cream together the softened butter, ricotta cheese, and granulated sugar using a hand or stand mixer. Beat until the mixture is light and fluffy, about 2–3 min.

Add the egg and vanilla extract, mixing until fully incorporated.

In a separate medium bowl, whisk together the flour, baking powder, and salt.

Gradually add the dry ingredients to the wet ingredients, mixing on low speed until just combined. Be careful not to overmix.

Gently fold in the mini chocolate chips using a spatula. The dough will be soft but manageable.

Drop tablespoon-sized scoops of dough onto the prepared baking sheets, spacing them about 2 inches apart to allow for spreading.

Use the back of a spoon or your fingers to gently flatten each cookie slightly.

Bake in the preheated oven for 12–15 minutes, or until the edges are lightly golden and the tops are set. For soft and chewy cookies, avoid overbaking.

Allow the cookies to cool on the baking sheet for 3 minutes before transferring them to a wire rack to cool completely.

Once the cookies are completely cool, dust them generously with powdered sugar.

Use whole-milk ricotta cheese for the best flavor and texture. Drain any excess liquid by pressing it through a fine-mesh sieve before measuring.

Substitute mini chocolate chips with chopped pistachios or candied orange peel for a more traditional cannoli flavor.

Cookies can be stored in an airtight container at room temperature for up to 3 days. Add a fresh dusting of powdered sugar before serving if needed.

Baked cookies can be pre frozen in a single layer, then transferred to a freezer-safe bag or container for up to 3 months. Thaw at room temperature and dust with powdered sugar before serving.

Pumpkin Chocolate Chip Cookies
(Submitted by Johanna Friesen)

Ingredients:
    1/2 cup butter - softened
    1/2 cup coconut milk
    3/4 cup dark brown sugar - packed
    3/4 cup light brown sugar - packed
    1 egg
    1 teaspoon vanilla extract
    2 cups flour
    1-1/2 cups quick-cooking oats
    1 teaspoon baking soda
    1 teaspoon ground cinnamon
    1 teaspoon pumpkin pie spice
    1 -1/2 cups cooked or canned pumpkin
    1-1/2 cups semisweet, dark, white, or butterscotch baking
chips

Directions:
    In a large mixing bowl, cream the butter, coconut milk, and sugars. Beat in egg and vanilla.
    In a medium mixing bowl, combine the flour, oats, baking soda, cinnamon, and pumpkin pie spice.
    Stir the dry mixture into the creamed mixture, alternately with pumpkin.
    Fold in baking chips of choice.
    Drop by tablespoonfuls onto greased baking sheets. Bake at 350° for 12-15 minutes, or until lightly browned.
    Yields 3 dozen cookies.

Raspberry Swirl Cookies
(Submitted by Patti Rusk)

Buttery, melt-in-your-mouth raspberry swirl cookies that are soft, a little chewy in the center, and have a ribbon of tangy-sweet raspberry jam!

Ingredients:

1 cup (2 sticks) unsalted butter, softened to room temperature

3/4 cup granulated sugar

1 large egg yolk

1 teaspoon pure vanilla extract

2 1/4 cups all-purpose flour

1/4 teaspoon salt

1/3 cup seedless raspberry jam

Optional: A little lemon zest (about 1 teaspoon)

Directions:

In a large mixing bowl, cream the softened butter and sugar together until light and fluffy.

Add egg yolk and vanilla extract. Mix until fully combined.

Add flour and salt. Mix just until a dough forms—it'll be soft but not sticky. If it's too crumbly, add a teaspoon of milk to bring it together.

On a lightly floured surface, press the dough into a rough rectangle (about 1/4 inch thick).

Spread a light layer of raspberry jam evenly over the dough, leaving about a 1/2-inch border.

Carefully roll the dough into a log, like you're making cinnamon rolls. It's okay if some jam squishes out! Wrap the log tightly in plastic wrap and chill in the fridge for at least 2 hours (or overnight if you're prepping ahead).

Preheat your oven to 350°. Line a baking sheet with parchment paper.

Slice the log into 1/4 to 1/2-inch cookies and place them about 2 inches apart on the sheet. Bake for 10–12 minutes, or until the edges are just barely golden. Don't overbake. These are meant to be soft! Cool on the pan for a few minutes before transferring to a wire rack.

Tips:

Use seedless jam for the smoothest swirls and best slicing.

If your dough is too soft to roll, pop it in the fridge for 10 minutes and try again. Want crispier edges? Sprinkle a little coarse sugar on the cookies right before baking. Feeling fancy? Drizzle with white chocolate once they've cooled!

Storage: Keep in an airtight container at room temp for up to 5 days

Freezer tip: You can freeze the uncooked dough log—just wrap it in foil and pop it in a zip-top bag. Slice and bake straight from the freezer (add 1-2 minutes to bake time).

Prep Time: 20 minutes (plus 2 hours chill time)

Cook Time: 10-12 minutes per batch

Fresh Apple Cake
(Submitted by Lena Winfrey Hayat)

Ingredients:
- 1 cup vegetable oil
- 2 cups sugar
- 3 eggs
- 2 cups self-rising flour
- 3 cups chopped fresh apples
- 1 cup chopped pecans
- 1 cup raisins
- 1 teaspoon cinnamon
- 1 teaspoon nutmeg
- 1 teaspoon vanilla

Directions:

Combine sugar and oil and beat well.

Add flour and beat well. Add remaining ingredients; stir to blend.

Bake in a well-greased tube pan or regular pan at 350 degrees for 45 to 50 minutes.

Cherry Bell Christmas Cookies
(Submitted by Kim Davis from
Cinnamon and Sugar and a Little Bit of Murder)

Ingredients:

Cookies:

3/4 cup unsalted butter, room temperature

1/2 cup granulated sugar

1 egg yolk

1 teaspoon almond extract

1/2 teaspoon sea salt

1-3/4 cup all-purpose flour

12 maraschino cherries, halved, patted dry

Icing (optional)

1/2 cup + 2 tablespoons confectioners' sugar

1/2 teaspoon meringue powder (optional)

2 teaspoons cool water

Directions:

In the bowl of a stand mixer, beat the butter on medium speed until creamy. Add in the granulated sugar and beat until the mixture is light and fluffy, about 3 minutes.

Beat in the egg yolk and almond extract.

Turn the mixer to low and mix in the salt and the flour, scraping down the sides of the bowl as needed. Mix just until combined.

Form the dough into a disk and wrap with plastic wrap. Refrigerate for at least 4 hours or overnight.

Allow the dough to sit at room temperature for 30 to 45 minutes, then preheat the oven to 375 degrees (F).

Line 2 baking sheets with parchment paper.

Roll the dough out on a well-floured surface to 1/8- to 1/4-

inch thick, and using a cookie cutter, cut into 2-1/2 to 3-inch rounds. Transfer onto the prepared baking sheets. Reroll scraps and repeat the process two times.

To form the rounds of dough into bell shapes, fold two edges of the upper half of the cookie over to the middle, overlapping somewhat. The top of the cookie should be narrow, and the bottom half should be wide. Refrigerate the shaped cookies on the baking sheet for 10 minutes, then place the halved cherries on the wide bottom half, just below the fold, to resemble a bell clapper.

Bake the cookies for 10 to 12 minutes, until the edges are barely golden brown. Remove from the oven and allow to cool on the baking sheet for 5 minutes, then transfer to a wire rack to cool completely.

Icing:

Stir the confectioners' sugar, meringue powder (if using), and the water together until completely smooth. You want the icing to be thick. Place the icing into a piping bag fitted with a size 3 round tip.

Outline the completely cooled cookies to resemble a bell, leaving the center fold line un-iced. Allow the icing to dry for at least 8 hours to harden.

Store leftover cookies in an airtight container with waxed or parchment paper between the layers at room temperature for up to three days.

Potato Chip Cookies
(Submitted by Petrenia Etheridge)

Ingredients:
  1 cup brown sugar
  1 cup white sugar
  1 cup shortening
  2 eggs
  1 teaspoon vanilla
  1/4 teaspoon salt
  1 teaspoon baking soda
  2 cups flour
  2 cups oatmeal
  2 cups crushed potato chips
  1 cup chopped pecans or walnuts

Directions:

Cream together sugars and shortening. Add eggs and vanilla.

Sift together flour, salt and soda and add to sugar mixture. Fold in oatmeal, chips, and nuts.

Spoon onto greased cookie sheet and bake at 375 for 10-15 minutes. This would be a good one to substitute gluten-free flour also.

Chocolate Truffles
(Submitted by Kim Davis from
Cinnamon and Sugar and a Little Bit of Murder)

Ingredients:
 Truffles:
 1 14-ounce sweetened condensed milk
 16 ounces good-quality bittersweet chocolate chips or bars chopped
 into small pieces
 2 teaspoons vanilla extract
 1 teaspoon ground cinnamon
 1/4 teaspoon sea salt
Garnish:
Your choice of cocoa powder, hot cocoa mix, non-melting confectioners' sugar, or holiday-themed candy sprinkles

Directions:
Heat the sweetened condensed milk in a small saucepan just until the edges start to bubble. Don't bring to a boil.

Place the chocolate in a medium-sized, heat-proof bowl. Pour the hot milk over the chocolate and allow to sit for two minutes. Add the vanilla, sea salt, and cinnamon, and stir until the chocolate is fully melted.

Cover and refrigerate until chilled, around 1 hour.

Roll the chilled mixture into small balls, and then roll into your choice of garnish.

Serve truffles at room temperature. Store leftovers in the refrigerator.

Fruitcake Cookies
(Submitted by Petrenia Etheridge)

Ingredients:
    1 cup shortening or butter
    1/4 teaspoon nutmeg
    1/4 teaspoon cinnamon
    Pinch of salt
    3 eggs
    2 1/2 cups cake flour
    2 cups walnuts, chopped
    2 cups pecans, chopped
    1 cup orange slices, chopped
    1 cup candied cherries, chopped
    2 cups candied pineapple, chopped
    1 1/2 cups raisins
    1 1/2 cups sugar
    1 teaspoon vanilla
    1 teaspoon baking soda

Directions:
Cream shortening and sugar, add eggs, nutmeg, cinnamon, and vanilla.

Add baking soda, salt, and flour.

Mix well, then fold in all the fruit and nuts.

Drop by teaspoons on greased cookie sheet and bake at 350 for 10-12 minutes.

First Day of School Cookies
(Submitted by Shelia Hall)

Ingredients:

    1 cup butter-flavored Crisco
    1 cup brown sugar
    ½ cup white sugar
    2 eggs
    1 teaspoon vanilla
    1 teaspoon salt
    1 teaspoon baking soda
    2½ cups flour
    1 cup chocolate chips
    1½ cups M&Ms

Directions:

    Cream Crisco and sugars together. Beat in eggs and vanilla.
    Add dry ingredients and mix well. Stir in chocolate chips
and M&Ms.
    Drop by spoonfuls onto an ungreased baking sheet.
    Bake at 350°F for 8–10 minutes.

Gingerbread Snowball Cookies
(Submitted by Patti Rusk)

Ingredients:
  1 cup butter, softened
  3/4 cup confectioner's sugar
  2 tablespoons molasses
  1 teaspoon vanilla extract
  2-1/4 cups all-purpose flour
  1 teaspoon cinnamon
  1 teaspoon ginger
  1/2 teaspoon nutmeg
  1/2 teaspoon cloves

For coating
  3/4 cup confectioner's sugar
  1/2 teaspoon cinnamon
  1/8 teaspoon ginger

Directions:
Preheat oven to 350°F. Line a baking sheet with parchment paper or a silicone mat.

In a large bowl cream together butter and confectioner's sugar until light and fluffy.

Add in the molasses and vanilla extract and beat until combined and creamy.

In a separate bowl, whisk together the flour, cinnamon, ginger, nutmeg, and cloves.

Add the dry ingredients into the wet ingredients, mixing until the dough comes together. The dough may seem crumbly but will hold when pressed.

Roll dough into 1" balls and place them on the prepared baking sheet about 2 inches apart.

Bake for 9-11 minutes, until the bottoms of the cookies are lightly browned. Let the cookies cool on the baking sheet for 2-4 minutes.

While the cookies are still warm, whisk together confectioner's sugar, cinnamon, and ginger for the coating. Roll the cookies in the sugar mixture until well coated.

Allow the cookies to cool completely on a wire rack. If needed, give them another roll in the sugar mixture if the coating has melted into the cookies.

Store leftovers in an airtight container.

Prep Time: 15 minutes

Baking Time: 9-11 minutes

Makes 36 cookies

Christmas Butter Cookies
(Submitted by Patti Rusk)

Ingredients:
    1/2 cup (1 stick) salted butter, softened
    1 8-oz cream cheese, softened
    1-1/2 cups granulated sugar
    1 large egg, room temperature
    1 teaspoon vanilla extract
    2-1/4 cups all-purpose flour
    1 cup confectioners' sugar, divided
    3 teaspoons baking powder
    1/3 cup Christmas sprinkles

Directions:

Preheat oven to 350°F. Line baking sheets with parchment paper.

In a large bowl using mixer, beat butter, cream cheese and granulated sugar until blended. Add in egg and vanilla.

Add in flour, baking powder, and ½ cup confectioners' sugar. With the mixer on low, gradually beat into the creamed mixture.

Gently fold in the sprinkles until just incorporated.

Using a 2-tablespoon cookie scoop, scoop dough. Roll each in the remaining ½ cup of confectioners' sugar. Place approximately 6 dough balls on each of the lined baking sheets. Using the bottom of a glass slightly flatten each dough ball.

Bake for 8-11 minutes, or until the tops of the cookies no longer appear wet.

Let the cookies rest for about 5 minutes before transferring onto a wire rack to cool completely.

Makes: 24 cookies

Peanut Butter Chocolate Chip Cookies
(Submitted by Brenda Ellis)

Ingredients:
    2-1/2 cups flour
    1 teaspoon baking soda
    1 teaspoon baking powder
    1 teaspoon salt
    1 stick of unsalted butter, melted
    3/4 cup peanut butter
    1/2 cup granulated sugar
    1 cup dark brown sugar
    2 eggs + 1 yolk
    2 teaspoons vanilla
    2 cups semisweet mini chips

Directions:
    Preheat oven to 350.
    Mix dry ingredients together.
    Mix wet ingredients together and combine well with dry mixture.
    Roll dough into balls and put onto cookie sheets.
    Bake for 12 minutes and cool for 5 minutes

Peanut Butter Snowballs
(Submitted by Colleen Galster)

Ingredients:
    2 cups powdered sugar
    1-1/3 cups peanut butter of your choice
    1/4 cup butter, melted
    2/3 cups graham cracker crumbs
    1 tablespoon maple syrup
    1 teaspoon salt
    2 teaspoons coconut oil
    2 cups white chocolate
    Sprinkles or garnish of choice

Directions:

Line baking sheet with parchment paper. Mix powdered sugar, peanut butter, graham cracker crumbs, butter, maple syrup, and salt in a large bowl with whisk until smooth.

Form into balls and place on baking sheet.

Combine melted white chocolate and coconut oil in a bowl until smooth. Dip the balls into the mix and then place on cooling rack to drip.

Top with sprinkles or garnish of choice and refrigerate about 15 minutes.

Orange Cranberry Ricotta Cookies
(Submitted by Alma Collins)

Ingredients:

    2 cups all-purpose flour

    1 teaspoon baking powder

    1/2 teaspoon salt

    1/2 cup unsalted butter, softened

    1 cup granulated sugar

    1 egg

    1 cup ricotta cheese (whole milk or part-skim)

    Zest of 1 orange

    2 tablespoons fresh orange juice

    1 cup dried cranberries

    Powdered sugar for dusting (optional)

Directions:

Preheat oven to 350°F (175°C) and line baking sheets with parchment paper.

In a medium bowl, whisk together flour, baking powder, and salt. Set aside.

In a large bowl, beat the butter and sugar until light and fluffy.

Add the egg and ricotta cheese, mixing until well combined. Stir in the orange zest and juice.

Gradually add the dry ingredients to the wet mixture, stirring until just combined.

Fold in the dried cranberries, then drop rounded tablespoons of dough onto the prepared baking sheets, leaving space between each cookie.

Bake for 12-15 minutes or until the edges are lightly golden. Let cool on a wire rack before dusting with powdered sugar if desired.

Nana's Kitchen Sink Cookies
(Submitted by Lanette Fields)

Ingredients:
  1-1/2 cups creamy peanut butter
  1/2 cup softened butter
  2 cups packed dark brown sugar
  1 tablespoon vanilla extract
  3 eggs
  4 cups quick-cook oats
  2 teaspoons baking soda
  1/2 cup butterscotch chips
  1/2 cup mini M&Ms
  1/2 cup semisweet chocolate chips
  1/2 cup white chocolate chips

Directions:

In a large mixing bowl, cream peanut butter, softened butter, and brown sugar. Add eggs one at a time, beating well after adding each egg. Beat in vanilla.

Add chips 1/2 cup at a time, mixing well after each addition. Add baking soda and mix in thoroughly.

Using a cookie scoop, drop onto parchment-lined cookie sheet.

Bake at 325 on a convection setting (or 350 at regular setting) for about 11 minutes or until edges are slightly brown. Cool on cookie sheet.

Snowy Winter Moons
(Submitted by Betty Rufledt)

Ingredients:
    1 cup butter, softened
    1 3/4 cups powdered sugar, divided
    1 egg
    1 teaspoon vanilla
    1 teaspoon almond extract
    2-1/4 cups flour
    1 teaspoon baking soda
    1 teaspoon cream of tartar
    3/4 cup jam, any flavor

Directions:

In large bowl, blend butter, 1-1/2 cups powdered sugar, egg, and extracts.

In separate bowl, combine flour, baking soda and cream of tartar; add to butter mixture. Cover dough; chill for 2 hours.

Preheat oven to 375 degrees. Divide dough in half; roll each half on lightly floured surface to 1/4 inches. Cut with 2-1/2 inch round cookie cutter. Place 1/2 teaspoon jam just off-center; fold over to create half-moon shape, pressing to seal edges. Place on parchment-lined cookie sheet. Bake for 7 to 8 minutes. Cool slightly and dust with powdered sugar. Makes about 5 dozen.

Recipe Notes

Recipe Notes

Recipe Notes

Acknowledgments

The expression "it takes a village" applies to many things, and writing a book is certainly one of them. *Sleigh Bells at Moonglow* only exists because of Annie Sarac's top-notch editing, which always makes a story shine, Elizabeth Christy's rope of developmental support when I fell into plot holes and needed help to climb out, Paul Sterrett's unwavering encouragement, and the efforts of many others who helped with various tasks along the way. The beautiful cover is thanks to the artistic talents of Mariah Sinclair. I'm also grateful to the Georgetown Writers for their constant encouragement.

As with other books in the Moonglow Christmas Series, Betty's cookie exchange gathers not only fictional treats but also recipes from readers. This year's delicious recipes are thanks to Lena Winfrey Hayat, Kay McCarter Pflueger, Annie Sarac, Petrenia Etheridge, Patti Rusk, Johanna Friesen, Kim Davis, Shelia Hall, Brenda Ellis, Colleen Galster, Alma Collins, Lanette Fields, and Betty Rufledt. What are you waiting for? Grab your kitchen apron and let's get baking!

Books by Deborah Garner

The Paige MacKenzie Series

Above the Bridge

When NY reporter Paige MacKenzie arrives in Jackson Hole, it's not long before her instincts tell her there's more than a basic story to be found in the popular, northwestern Wyoming mountain area. A chance encounter with attractive cowboy Jake Norris soon has Paige chasing a legend of buried treasure passed down through generations. Sidestepping a few shady characters who are also searching for the same hidden reward, she will have to decide who is trustworthy and who is not.

The Moonglow Café

The discovery of an old diary inside the wall of the historic hotel soon sends NY reporter Paige MacKenzie into the underworld of art and deception. Each of the town's residents holds a key to untangling more than one long-buried secret, from the hippie chick owner of a new age café to the mute homeless man in the town park. As the worlds of western art and sapphire mining collide, Paige finds herself juggling research, romance, and danger.

Three Silver Doves

The New Mexico resort of Agua Encantada seems a perfect destination for reporter Paige MacKenzie to combine work with well-deserved rest and relaxation. But when suspicious jewelry shows up on another guest, and the town's storyteller goes missing, Paige's R&R is soon redefined as restlessness and risk. Will an unexpected overnight trip to Tierra Roja Casino lead her to the answers she seeks, or are darker secrets lurking along the way?

Hutchins Creek Cache

When a mysterious 1920s coin is discovered behind the Hutchins Creek Railroad Museum in Colorado, Paige MacKenzie starts digging into four generations of Hutchins family history, with a little help from the Denver Mint. As legends of steam engines and coin mintage mingle, will Paige discover the true origin of the coin, or will she find herself riding the rails dangerously close to more than one long-hidden town secret?

Crazy Fox Ranch

As Paige MacKenzie returns to Jackson Hole, she has only two things on her mind: enjoy life with Wyoming's breathtaking Grand Tetons as the backdrop and spend more time with handsome cowboy Jake Norris as he prepares to open his guest ranch. But when a stranger's odd behavior leads her to research Western filming in the area—in particular, the movie Shane, will it simply lead to a freelance article for the Manhattan Post, or will it lead to a dangerous, hidden secret?

Sweet Sierra Gulch

Paige MacKenzie isn't convinced there's anything "sweet" about Sweet Sierra Gulch when she arrives in the small California Gold Rush town. Still, there's plenty of history as well as anticipated romance with her favorite cowboy, Jake Norris. But when the owner of the local café goes missing, Paige is determined to find out why. Will she uncover a dangerous secret in the town's old mining tunnels, or will curiosity land her in over her head?

The Sadie Kramer Flair Series

A Flair for Chardonnay

When flamboyant senior sleuth Sadie Kramer learns the owner of her favorite chocolate shop is in trouble, she heads for the California wine country with a tote-bagged Yorkie and a slew of questions. The fourth generation Tremiato Winery promises answers, but not before a dead body turns up at the vintners' scheduled Harvest Festival. As Sadie juggles truffles, tips, and turmoil, she'll need to sort the grapes from the wrath in order to find the identity of the killer.

A Flair for Drama

When a former schoolmate invites Sadie Kramer to a theatre production, she jumps at the excuse to visit the Monterey Bay area for a weekend. Plenty of action is expected on stage, but when the show's leading lady turns up dead, Sadie finds herself faced with more than one drama to follow. With both cast members and production crew as potential suspects, will Sadie and her sidekick Yorkie, Coco, be able to solve the case?

A Flair for Beignets

With fabulous music, exquisite cuisine, and rich culture, how could a week in New Orleans be anything less than fantastic for Sadie Kramer and her sidekick Yorkie, Coco? And it is... until a customer at a popular patisserie drops dead face-first in a raspberry-almond tart. A competitive bakery, a newly formed friendship, and even her hotel's luxurious accommodations offer possible suspects. As Sadie sorts through a gumbo of interconnected characters, will she discover who the killer is, or will the killer discover her first?

A Flair for Truffles

Sadie Kramer's friendly offer to deliver three boxes of gourmet Valentine's Day truffles for her neighbor's chocolate shop backfires when she arrives to find the intended recipient deceased. Even more intriguing is the fact that the elegant heart-shaped gifts were ordered by three different men. With the help of one detective and the hindrance of another, Sadie will search San Francisco for clues. But will she find out "whodunit" before the killer finds a way to stop her?

A Flair for Flip-Flops

When the body of a heartthrob celebrity washes up on the beach outside Sadie Kramer's luxury hotel suite, her fun in the sun soon turns into sleuthing with the stars. The resort's wine and appetizer gatherings, suspicious guest behavior, and casual strolls along the beach boardwalk may provide clues, but will they be enough to discover who the killer is, or will mystery and mayhem leave a Hollywood scandal unsolved?

A Flair for Goblins

When Sadie Kramer agrees to help decorate for San Francisco's high-society Halloween shindig, she expects to find whimsical ghosts, skeletons, and jack-o-lanterns when she shows up at the Wainwright Mansion—not a body. With two detectives, a paranormal investigator turned television star, and a cauldron full of family members cackling around her, Sadie and her sidekick Yorkie are determined to find out who the killer is. Will an old superstition help lead to the truth? Or will this simply become one more tale in the mansion's haunted history?

A Flair for Shamrocks

When flamboyant senior sleuth Sadie Kramer's car breaks down outside a small Oregon beach town, the repair lands her in unexpected lodging above an Irish pub for St. Patrick's Day. With pub games, green beer, and a potbellied pig named Paddy in the mix, it's bound to be a unique holiday. But not all is what it seems in Irishton, especially when the owner of the pub turns up dead. An assortment of local characters could be guilty, but only one is the killer. Sadie and her sidekick Yorkie will need the luck of the Irish to solve the mystery.

A Flair for Vegas

When Sadie Kramer meets up with her friend Myrtle for a girls' getaway in Las Vegas, they're especially thrilled when VIP tickets to the hotel's sold-out production of *Bugsy's Juice Joint* unexpectedly fall into their hands. That is until the body of the show's director is found in his hotel room and the show is postponed. With suspects spread throughout the hotel, casino, and theater, Sadie and Myrtle have some sleuthing to do. Add in Coco's typical Yorkie antics, and it's bound to be a weekend no one will forget. Will Sadie manage to solve this mystery? Or will what happens in Vegas stay in Vegas?

The Moonglow Christmas Series

Mistletoe at Moonglow

The small town of Timberton, Montana, hasn't been the same since resident chef and artist, Mist, arrived, bringing a unique new age flavor to the old western town. When guests check in for the holidays, they bring along worries, fears, and broken hearts, unaware that Mist has a way of working magic in people's lives. One thing is certain: no matter how cold winter's grip is on each guest, no one leaves Timberton without a warmer heart.

Silver Bells at Moonglow

Christmas brings an eclectic gathering of visitors and locals to the Timberton Hotel each year, guaranteeing an eventful season. Add in a hint of romance, and there's more than snow in the air around the small Montana town. When the last note of Christmas carols has faded away, the soft whisper of silver bells from the front door's wreath will usher guests and townsfolk back into the world with hope for the coming year.

Gingerbread at Moonglow

The Timberton Hotel boasts an ambiance of near-magical proportions during the Christmas season. As the aromas of ginger, cinnamon, nutmeg, and molasses mix with heartfelt camaraderie and sweet romance, holiday guests share reflections on family, friendship, and life. Will decorating the outside of a gingerbread house prove easier than deciding what goes inside?

Nutcracker Sweets at Moonglow

When a nearby theater burns down just before Christmas, cast members of *The Nutcracker* arrive at the Timberton Hotel with only a sliver of holiday joy. Camaraderie, compassion, and shared inspiration combine to help at least one hidden dream come true. As with every Christmas season, this year's guests will face the New Year with a renewed sense of hope.

Snowfall at Moonglow

As holiday guests arrive at the Timberton Hotel with hopes of a white Christmas, unseasonably warm weather hints at a less-than-wintery wonderland. But whether the snow falls or not, one thing is certain: with resident artist and chef, Mist, around, there's bound to be a little magic. No one ever leaves Timberton without renewed hope for the future.

Yuletide at Moonglow

When a Yuletide festival promises jovial crowds, resident artist and chef, Mist, knows she'll have her hands full. Between the legendary Christmas Eve dinner at the Timberton Hotel and this season's festival events, the unique magic of Christmas in this small Montana town offers joy, peace, and community to guests and townsfolk alike. As always, no one will return home without a renewed sense of hope for the future.

Starlight at Moonglow

As the Christmas holiday approaches, a blizzard threatens the peaceful ambiance that the Timberton Hotel usually offers its guests. Even resident artist and chef, Mist, known to work near miracles, has no control over the howling winds and heavy snowfall. But there's always a bit of magic in this small Montana town, and this year's storm may just find it's no match for heartfelt camaraderie, joyful inspiration, and sweet romance.

Joy at Moonglow

Each holiday season is unique in the small Montana town of Timberton. New and returning guests bring their dreams, cares, and worries, and always leave with lighter hearts and renewed hope for the future. But no season has ever been as special as this one. Because, to everyone's delight, wedding bells will be ringing. Thanks to the heartfelt efforts of many and no shortage of sweet romance, this year will be the most joyful of all.

Evergreen Wishes at Moonglow

Christmas in the small town of Timberton, Montana, is always filled with holiday traditions, exquisite cuisine, and heartfelt camaraderie. When a majestic evergreen tree is placed in the center of town, inviting ornaments containing wishes, townsfolk and visitors are soon pondering what their hopes and dreams might be. Although wishes can't always come true, some just might with a bit of holiday magic.

Angels at Moonglow

The small Montana town of Timberton always provides a joyful Christmas retreat for visitors as well as those who live in the area. This year, an angel ornament project offers guests and local townsfolk a chance to reflect on others in their lives. As always, time spent together, exquisite food, and camaraderie allow guests a chance to trade worries for a sense of peace and hope for the future.

Sleigh Bells at Moonglow

Christmas in the small Montana town of Timberton is always filled with wonder as well as heartfelt camaraderie, exquisite cuisine, and holiday cheer. An old-fashioned sleigh ride through the forest this year promises to add plenty of joy for both visitors and townsfolk. Add to that the traditional Christmas Eve feast, the yearly cookie exchange, and resident artist and chef Mist's unique way of bringing inspiration to the season, and it's guaranteed to be a holiday to cherish.

For more information on Deborah Garner's books:

Facebook: https://www.facebook.com/deborahgarnerauthor

Twitter: https://twitter.com/PaigeandJake

Website: http://deborahgarner.com

Mailing list: http://eepurl.com/bj-clD